The Ladies
from
St. Petersburg

The Ladies
from
St. Petersburg

THREE NOVELLAS BY

Nina Berberova

TRANSLATED BY
MARIAN SCHWARTZ

A NEW DIRECTIONS BOOK

Book design by Sylvia Frezzolini Severance
Manufactured in the United States of America
New Directions Books are printed on acid-free paper
First published clothbound by New Directions in 1998
Published simultaneously in Canada by Penguin Books Canada Limited

Library of Congress Cataloging-in-Publication Data
Berberova, Nina Nikolaevna.
    [Novels. English. Selections]
    The ladies from St. Petersburg / Nina Berberova ; translated by
Marian Schwartz.
        p.   cm.
    Contents: The ladies from St. Petersburg—Zoya Andreyevna—The
big city.
    ISBN 0-8112-1377-3 (alk. paper)
    1. Berberova, Nina Nikolaevna—Translations into English.
I. Schwartz, Marian.   II. Title.
PG3476.B425A28   1998
891.73'42—dc21   98-18968
                                                          CIP

New Directions Books are published for James Laughlin
By New Directions Publishing Corporation
80 Eighth Avenue, New York 10011

SECOND PRINTING

Contents

Foreword

Born in 1901, Berberova witnessed an historical period and an historical generation so remote that they have long since entered our realm of imagination. Indeed, she attended Alexander Blok's funeral in 1921. For over seventy years, first in Europe and then in America, Berberova wrote and published steadily, unknown outside a very small circle of Russian readers. She published her first work in English— her autobiography, *The Italics Are Mine*—in 1969, and eighteen years passed before she published the next.

Literature was both cause and effect in Berberova's life. In Europe, in the 1920s and 1930s, when finances were always precarious, Berberova produced a steady stream of stories, poems, and reviews for the Russian press of Paris and Europe. During her long career, she wrote every kind of fiction and nonfiction—biographies, novels, novellas, short stories, plays, reviews, and straight journalism—as well as poetry. She met poet and critic Vladislav Khodasevich as a consequence of her writing—having submitted poems in application to the House of Writers in Petrograd—and fell in love with him. Together they participated in the literary life of Petrograd, the former St. Petersburg, until emigrating in 1922. Berberova lived in Berlin, Prague, and Italy before settling down in Paris with Khodasevich, whom she eventually left, and then later with a second "husband," a Russian painter. However, when I first met Berberova, people referred to her as "Khodasevich's wife," and no matter how much time had passed and what their personal problems, she didn't seem to mind this label. She knew him as a great writer and was proud of the association, and she could laugh at the stodgy old Russian professors trying to pigeon-hole her.

Berberova was the classic "neglected writer," which is to say that despite her literary excellence, readers and critics overlooked her, mostly due to circumstances beyond her control (revolution, war, social prejudice). Yet, unlike so many others who have suffered that fate, she lived to relish her resurrection and vindication. Berberova died in 1993, a professor emeritus at Princeton University and a celebrity and best-selling author in France and Russia—her status attesting to the force of her art, her intellect, and her will. In 1985, the French firm Actes Sud published Berberova's *L'Accompagnatrice*, which went on to become a best-seller (and later a film), the first of a string of best-sellers for her in French translation. Whenever Berberova visited Paris from the late 1980s on, she toured as a celebrity. A friend of mine brought back a snapshot she had taken of a Paris bookstore's display window devoted exclusively to Berberova titles. Berberova herself said that she knew she had "made it" when *Le Monde* quoted her and they didn't have to explain who she was. The irony of her "discovery" in France, where she had lived in obscurity for over twenty years, did not escape her.

Berberova witnessed Communism's triumph and its agony. When Gorbachev came to power and declared glasnost and then perestroika, Berberova got her hopes up, perhaps for the first time since her emigration. She then rode an emotional roller coaster following the downfall of Communism and the succession of publishing milestones, as Russia reclaimed its writers. Khodasevich's work came out. When her turn came, the Soviet houses published her in vast quantities. She had finally reached the principal Russian reading public, her primary reader. To her, nothing else mattered so much.

I met Berberova in the early 1980s, when I had begun to translate one of her nonfiction books. Berberova had been a small, slim woman of striking beauty all her life, and a good deal of her intense self-esteem derived from her belief in her own attractiveness. In her eighties, when I first knew her, her vanity—a term that in her case had positive connotations—kept her vigorous, physically and mentally. I had been warned that she did not suffer fools gladly,

but she took a liking to me that expressed itself not
only in appreciation for my professional abilities but
also in disapproval that I did not care one whit about
my graying hair and that I thought I could have children and a career, a premise she never accepted. She
was not shy about speaking her mind. Toward the
end of her life, as if she knew time was increasingly
precious, she became more impatient than ever and a
few times simply hung up in the middle of a telephone call if I ran out of interesting conversation.
There were no hard feelings; she was simply too busy
to be bored. In the decade or so of our collaboration, I
would call her periodically and arrange a visit, which
always followed a precise timetable: pickup from the
train at Princeton Junction in the late morning, a
walk through Princeton to the Faculty Club for
lunch, back to her house for dessert, a brief nap in the
yard if she could talk me into it, and then work, side
by side at her dining table, on the current text.

After I had worked on that first project for a
while and it dawned on me how fine a writer she was,
I innocently inquired one day whether she had ever
written fiction. Indeed she had written a substantial

amount, beginning with her Billancourt stories, published in the 1920s in the Russian emigré press—chronicles of the lives of the now working-class Russian refugees who had settled in Billancourt, where they worked for the most part at the Renault plant. When I asked that question in 1982, however, her fiction had scarcely been reprinted, translated, or discussed, let alone taught. In any case, at that point in her life Berberova was immersed in history and felt ambivalent about fiction in general, including her own. Nonetheless, she pulled two texts off her shelf and gave them to me. The first, "The Big City"—perhaps her final story—was the one she felt least ambivalent about at the time; the other was the original Russian edition, published in Paris, of *Sentence Commuted*, a collection that formed the nucleus for *The Tattered Cloak and Other Novellas* (Knopf, 1991).

The Ladies from St. Petersburg is the fourth volume of Nina Berberova's fiction to appear in English and the first translated since her death in 1993. Together, the three stories in this volume—"The Ladies from St. Petersburg," "Zoya Andreyevna," and "The Big

City"—form a provocative ensemble. Chronologically, they frame the period for which most readers best know Berberova—the not small but highly circumscribed world of Russian emigrés of all classes in Paris between the two world wars. In the stories here, we have these same people but ante- and post-Paris. "The Ladies from St. Petersburg" and "Zoya Andreyevna" appear among her earliest stories, and "The Big City" may have been her last. We find the ladies from St. Petersburg at the very beginning of Russia's political turmoil, before people are using the word "revolution," an event that in this story has not yet coalesced, that directly affects but does not yet imperil their personal lives. This mother-daughter pair does not know that if they survive they will flee, probably to Paris but maybe to Shanghai or even South America. They have had glimpses of hardship but have not yet lost anything. They planned their vacation in the country well before the cloud of political disarray appeared on their narrow horizon. When she arrives, Margarita, the daughter, is still a girl, toying with her marital options; when she leaves, abruptly matured, she knows that marriage post-haste is her only choice.

The title character of the next story, Zoya Andreyevna, appeals to us much more—like Anna Karenina, an elegant, privileged, relatively young woman who has broken rigid sexual prohibitions, first by leaving a man because she no longer loved him, and then by living in sin. She has divorced a perfectly good husband and foolishly thrown away her social status for love. How ironic that her new landladies, no revolutionaries themselves and hostile to what the Bolsheviks bring, can only hate her all the more for her lost social and economic status and wish her ill. War, the great equalizer, has cast Zoya Andreyevna adrift, as it did so many women and children, without her male protector, who has joined the White Army. Like many others, Zoya Andreyevna is fleeing, staying one train ride ahead of the fighting, uncertain which compass point the next leg of her journey will take. In all likelihood, if she survives, she too will end up in Paris, in the emigré world more precarious than the city that sheltered it but stability itself compared to the milieu in "Zoya

Andreyevna" and "The Ladies from St. Petersburg." The protagonist in "The Big City" has fled twice, first to Europe and now, after the Second World War, to America. Though none of these people is Berberova, emigration defines major moments in their lives, as one could argue it did for her.

In "The Big City," Berberova presents very much her own vision of New York, when she arrived from Paris in 1950 with a few dollars in her pocket and scarcely a word of English. In this work of fiction, Berberova recreates the surreal impression that can result from the stranger's vantage. It captures the fragile moment when the new world seems opaque and the one left behind seems the most real. Because she and I addressed this story specifically, I can be certain that this "big city" is not an imaginary place but New York, even though she insisted on referring to Manhattan as a "cape" in the opening paragraph. In the Russian, Berberova seems to make another odd word choice, referring to the "lower town" and the "upper town" as if it were a matter of elevation, but she means only "downtown" and "uptown." One can easily see why she would have resisted using the

usual Russian term for "downtown"—*tsentr*—because, of course, downtown Manhattan has not been
the "center" for over a century.

Berberova spoke and wrote elegant, pre-revolutionary, Petersburg Russian, a language that now,
with her passing, has become rare if not extinct, pres-
ent-day Russian being to pre-Soviet Russian more or
less as Newspeak is to the King's English. No Russian intellectuals educated in pre-revolutionary Russia
survive. Berberova often pointed out the fact that she
belonged to the last generation fully educated in
Russia before the Revolution. Nabokov obtained his
higher education as a young man in England, of
course, but his Russian education, like Berberova's,
was by then complete. The Russian that Berberova
spoke and wrote held on tenaciously for decades inside the Soviet Union in the work of Bulgakov,
Pasternak, Akhmatova and in the spoken word of
their peers, but by now the language of fine literature
has changed. One finds the few living heirs to the
pre-revolutionary language mostly in Moscow, not
Petersburg. Contemporary Russian has not merely
evolved; it shows all too clearly the trauma of its

twentieth-century past. Not that Russian could freeze in emigration any more than it could at home. New situations constantly press for linguistic change, and Russian has undergone startling changes just since the fall of the Soviet Union. Berberova described the quandary of emigrés, isolated from the bulk of Russian speakers, trying to put a name to post-revolutionary phenomena: for example, they had used the word *gelikopter* initially, until they learned the Soviets' term, coined with a Slavic root— *vertolyot,* roughly, "vertical flyer."

I did not have the luxury of consulting with Berberova when I began to work on "Zoya Andreyevna" and "The Ladies from St. Petersburg," and I missed being able to call her up or arrange a visit to go over the texts. I felt like a fledgling she had pushed out of her nest. I was on my own. However, she had surely taught me enough so that I could answer most of my own questions, and I did. Nevertheless, some details may remain unknowable because no one survives to explain the realities of a very specific daily life vanished for too many decades.

Working with Berberova allowed me to tap into

this kind of privileged knowledge—for example, in "Astashev in Paris" in her *Tattered Cloak* collection. Astashev visits a fashionable Parisian neighborhood early in the morning, before the men of the family have left for work, and sees a maid walking what the Russian seems to call a blue sheepdog (*golubaia ovcharka*). When I expressed puzzlement at this image, Berberova proceeded to regale me on the subject of fashionable dogs owned by wealthy Russian emigrés in Paris between the wars. What they referred to as a "blue sheepdog" turned out to be a bluish-gray poodle with a shaved back. And in fact, she knew all about the canine sociology of her subjects, and chose her dogs carefully. The bereaved dog in "The Big City" is a borzoi, a dog that can convey nobility of spirit through its appearance as well as its behavior. This kind of telling detail was so important to Berberova's art that the translator must take special care to make these details as accurate as possible. For example, in the second sentence of "Zoya Andreyevna," Berberova describes her heroine as she arrives from the train, much the worse for her journey: "Her Assyrian feather had snapped and now hung down over her right ear; there were dark circles under her tired eyes, whether from the soot or exhaustion she didn't know, and the sleeve of her fur coat was coming out at the seam, allowing a clump of dirty wadding to escape." The symbolism of a snapped feather is straightforward. Yet what is an Assyrian feather, and what does it mean about Zoya Andreyevna that she wears one in her hat? And why in the Russian is the term spelled as it would be pronounced in French, *assyrie?* What exactly did Zoya Andreyevna's open-work stockings, mentioned later, look like, and did they imply she was brazen, merely fashion-conscious, or perhaps out-of-date due to her reduced circumstances? To take an example from another story, various carriages come up quite frequently in "The Ladies from St. Petersburg." We infer that the "tall gig" that appears in the first sentence is a modest rig because it is pulled by a single horse and used on provincial country roads, and the term Berberova uses for it, *pletyonka*, implies that some part of it was woven, perhaps the hood. I've often wondered, however, what associations this word evoked in Berberova's readers.

The two early stories revel in Berberova's genius for the particular, most of which we can fully appreciate. Even with all the insight we have lost over time, we can easily paint a picture of Varvara Ivanovna's funeral that would give a face to all in attendance, and the sound of the nasty dripping from her corpse still makes my stomach turn. We know precisely what aspect of the student's appearance and dress struck Zoya Andreyevna and informed her opinion of him. The closing scene, when the student takes Zoya Andreyevna away in the taxicab and is startled by the grotesque faces looking out of his landladies' window, is as vivid as a movie. As the years passed and her writing matured, Berberova used detail just as effectively but more sparingly, so that by the time we get to "The Big City" characters and locations have no names, and the protagonist's past and present circumstances are painted in a few strokes. The detail lies in the intense, moment-to-moment perceptions and in the philosophical conceits, and the entire plot turns on a drip of paint.

—*Marian Schwartz*

The Ladies
from
St. Petersburg

The Ladies
from
St. Petersburg

I

A tall gig harnessed to a broad-boned, long-maned mare stopped at the porch of a large country residence. The horse swished its tail high across the rising moon. Varvara Ivanovna and Margarita got busy with their bags: these were not times to be relying on servants. In the house, though, they had already sprung into action. Doors were opening, a reddish strip of light fell on the black lawn, and through that light two barefoot girls hurried toward the luggage. Dr. Byrdin and his wife came out on the porch.

Dr. Byrdin's "establishment" was located twelve

versts from the station. Just before the war, when construction on the branch line from Bologoe to Khomuty was finished, it had been considered no more than a six-hour trip by rail. Now, the ladies who had arrived from St. Petersburg were thoroughly exhausted. They had been traveling, it turned out, more than two full days, had not slept, and had changed trains three times. In Maksaty, the porter had hoisted Margarita right through the train car window. Before she could cry out she had been plunked down in a compartment packed with people and their belongings. Varvara Ivanovna pushed her way across the platform to the cursing of the crowd and the jeers of the soldiers who occupied the step of the next car—men on leave and deserters. When they got off at Khomuty, she tripped over the bodies of the women spread out in the corridor, their bundles, and their infants, from each and every one of whom a small puddle trickled.

The new arrivals were taken to the room they had had reserved since Easter. Varvara Ivanovna inspected the bed and the cleanliness of the towels hanging above the blue enamel washbasin and ran her finger along the top shelf of the closet. Without removing her coat, Margarita walked over to the open window.

The house was ringed by plane trees, and in the solid silence of the old garden the sky seemed very close indeed with all its stars and its full white moon, which was now swinging at the end of a fluffy cloud. A stretch of the lane was awash in the light that fell across Margarita's head, and black beetles had already started crawling on the windowsill.

In the garden, directly under the window, stood three maidenly white shadows. Their whispers were barely audible.

"So what is this happiness all about really?" asked one, the youngest, who was probably fifteen or so. She wore a blue sash tied under her bosom and her braids were pinned around her head.

"Oh, Verochka"—someone's voice trembled with agitation—"that's not something you can talk about. You have to experience it."

But Verochka piped up again, looking first at one and then the other of her friends: "You mean love? But love—that can't really be all there is to it? What's it supposed to be like then?"

"What terrific fools they are!" thought Margarita, and she moved away from the window.

She washed up after her mother and then took a good look at herself in the mirror. She tugged a bright red curl down on her forehead—a little less than she used to in Petersburg before the arrival of Leonid Leonidovich, but enough to give her quite a sophisticated look. She had a slim and well-proportioned figure and a high bosom—practically up to her shoulders.

Downstairs, on the balcony that led out to the garden, which was silvery black in the moonlight, dinner had been made ready for the new arrivals. A milk-white porcelain lamp cast a circle of light on the tablecloth, above which flitted dusty, night-loving moths. In the corners, by the white wooden columns, Dr. Byrdin's guests sat as if they had just chanced to wander in. All of them were robust, ruddy from the sun, and clumsy from their canvas slippers. The women, who had tired of one another long ago, pretended to be admiring the landscape from the balcony: the garden path and the jasmine bush. The rest was lost in the gloom. The men were preoccupied with storing their oars. These were not times to be leaving oars out in the open overnight.

"Pardon me, but I understand you're from Petersburg, is that right?" Rabinovich inquired politely when everyone had been introduced and Varvara Ivanovna, her pinkie extended, had turned her attention to the cold duck.

"Well, it looks as though I'm going to be the best one here," thought Margarita, and she rejoiced.

"It would be very interesting to learn if there were, by chance, any political news?"

"Do you mean you don't know? There's been an uprising in Petrograd!"

"That can't be! Oh my, do tell us all about it!"

Varvara Ivanovna smiled with seemly bitterness: "With pleasure. It all began on Monday the third. Yes, the third of July, isn't that right, Margarita? You couldn't buy anything. All the stores shut down at once. Imagine that!"

Everyone shook their heads.

"There was terrible shooting in the streets. The maximalists armed the workers from the Kschessinska mansion."

"Well, that's not all that frightening," said Dr. Byrdin, taking some tweezers from his pocket.

"Don't interrupt!" exclaimed Rabinovich. "Let madam speak. This is most interesting."

"We left on the fifth. Not all the trains were running by then, but our friends, well, you know, they positively insisted that we go. Naturally, I wasn't concerned for myself"—Varvara Ivanovna gave the ladies a look—"I was concerned for my Margaritochka."

The ladies made ingratiating faces.

"You understand, gentlemen, this was only a minor flare-up." Varvara Ivanovna was using other people's words, but she'd forgotten whose. "But a conflagration might break out any day now. I said that when the Democrats left the ministry." She popped a piece of cucumber into her mouth. "At that point it became perfectly clear to me that we were doomed."

Byrdin looked at her with lazy hostility.

"I trust, nonetheless, that such is by no means the case, gentle lady. I assure you that all this revolution business will fizzle out very quickly. We here are all

agreed that the Bolsheviks have no chance whatso-
ever of success."

"Nothing but a pack of Socialist extremists!" in-
terjected Rabinovich.

"Precisely. I know the people"—Byrdin's eyes
turned toward the animal yard, although from the
balcony all you could see there (even during the day)
was an old empty dog kennel—"I know our Russian
people, and for them their principal enemy right
now are the Germans."

Everyone exchanged glances. Rabinovich
coughed: "And how will this all end?" he asked again
as politely as possible.

"What can I tell you? On Wednesday it looked as
though matters were already taking a turn for the
calmer. . . ."

"There, you see!"

". . . and I think you'll be getting the newspapers in a couple of days."

She pushed her plate away, crossing her knife and
fork, and wiped her small, unattractive mouth.

"All this is very much appreciated. You'll never
learn anything from the newspapers."

Someone grunted smugly.

Margarita stood up and gaily rustled her silk underskirt. One of the ladies—skinny, wearing large earrings and a lace dress—stood up as well, leaned over the railing, and said slowly, in the direction of the garden: "Nevertheless, these are such frightening times, and what a trial for our young people!"

Everyone turned to look at her. Varvara Ivanovna paid close attention to her earrings and dress.

"Yes, yes, I'm mostly frightened for the young people," she said in her usual 'company' voice. "I'm not afraid of dying myself, I'm only afraid of Margaritochka being left without me."

The lady in the earrings straightened up.

"That's it precisely. You know, when my Verochka kept running out to Kamennoostrovsky Boulevard three times a day in February—well, I thought I would go mad."

"My God, how boring it's going to be here," thought Margarita.

Another lady, younger, a lisper, with a full head of curls, suddenly spoke up: "No, no, I'm afraid of dying myself. That's the most frightening thing of all. You do and what's there? All of a sudden—no one? Could anyone really bear that?"

"You're talking that way because you don't have children," said the first, nonchalantly.

Varvara Ivanovna picked two crumbs off her lap.

"Well, I'm not afraid of death," she said again. "And you know, I dearly love all these conversations about death." She seemed to be inviting everyone to speak up, but for some reason no one did and then somehow they all stood up at the same time. The doctor's wife cleared away the plates. In the doorway there was some confusion as they stepped back to let each other through. Finally, Varvara Ivanovna and Margarita found themselves in their own room.

"Such lovely, pleasant company," said Varvara Ivanovna. "And what a comfortable house!"

She hung up her blouses, rubbed cream into her hands, and began removing her corset, her face contorted and scarlet from exertion—the upper and then the lower hooks kept catching on the steel eyes.

"Well, it's going to be more fun for you than me," Margarita smiled as she wound her hair in curling papers. Her long nightgown smelled of food and her suitcase, and all these odors she had had to breathe for the last few hours were starting to make her feel sick. There was one smell, actually, releasing a memory that made her heart contract blissfully: the smell of the evening fields their peasant had driven them through on their long ride. This smell came from the warm earth, from the tall but green oats, and from the small round haystacks, which receded in rows into the even, green distance, where the sky, darkened with every verst, merged with the flat earth.

"Please, say your prayers," said Varvara Ivanovna, spreading her legs in order to remove her shoes.

"I would have, if you hadn't said something first."

Margarita lay down and flung the blanket back. It was a hot night. Suddenly she saw the light go out on the brass knobs of the bedposts; then the springs began creaking underneath Varvara Ivanovna.

"It's going to be impossible to sleep here," muttered Margarita as she drifted off. "It sounds like there's a bird singing right in the room."

"That's not a bird, it's a cricket, my dear. You'd better not say anything so foolish in public."

In the window there were stars and the tufts of trees.

II

Margarita woke up and, before she could figure out what had woken her, saw an inverted moon right at the windowsill, very red and bent. Something was keeping her from falling back to sleep.

"Mmm," moaned Varvara Ivanovna.

"Mama, is something the matter?"

The moan got louder and longer. It could probably be heard in the garden.

"Take it easy now." Margarita was scared. "Where did you put the matches?"

She fished her shoes out from under the bed with her bare feet, ran to the table with outstretched arms, and snatched up the matchbox. The candle's flame, the same color as the moon setting outside the window, began flickering in the room.

She saw her mother lying on her back, her pale eyes opened wide; perspiration and tears were running down her cheeks and lips. She was mewling, her left hand pointing first to her mouth, then to her immobile right flank.

Margarita leapt to her side with a cry and leaned over her mother's face but could not make out a single word through the ragged, labored mewling.

"Does it hurt?" she asked, and her curling papers fell into her eyes.

Varvara Ivanovna shook her head and pointed to the door.

"The doctor?"

Varvara Ivanovna nodded.

Margarita threw on her coat and ran out into the hall, leaving the door open. She saw a row of locked doors, ran as far as the staircase, and looked down. All was dark and quiet. She took a step back and, not knowing where the Byrdins' room was, prepared to raise a cry in the hall. What time could it be? Suddenly, under one of the doors, she saw a strip of light. She knocked softly and opened it. The light in the room went out instantly. Someone only a few paces away had blown out the candle.

"For the love of God forgive me. My mother's had an attack. Where is the doctor's room?"

Someone sat up in the bed and struck a match.

"I'll be right there. Come in. I was reading and I thought it was Mama. Only don't tell anyone or I'm in for it."

Margarita saw a small room and a bed and washbasin like her own. Skinny Verochka, her braids tied up in red ribbons, was scurrying around the room in her bare feet.

"Let's go, let's go quickly," she whispered, wrapping her robe around her and picking up the candleholder. "My God, this is horrible—and I was so frightened. I thought it was Mama. Sometimes she comes in and checks." Remembering something, she dashed back to the bed, pulled a thick book bound in red calico out from under the blanket, and shoved it under the mattress.

Both girls ran down the stairs. Verochka held her small, translucent, ink-stained hand in front of the candle to keep it from going out.

Several doors opened simultaneously. Puffy faces poked out into the hall. Something was going on in the room of the ladies who had arrived that evening from Petersburg, something that might well have gone on in the daytime but certainly had no business going on at night. Voices were coming from there— a man's, a woman's, a man's, a woman's. Then there was a brief silence. And then someone let out a scream that was heard all over the house, waking everyone who was not already awake. It was Margarita. She was all alone in the world now. Varvara Ivanovna was dying.

Varvara Ivanovna tried mightily to say something. At last Margarita put a small gold pencil and a scrap of stationery into her left hand, but it was too late. Not more than half an hour had elapsed between the first and second attack. The doctor, dressed only in his long underwear, had managed to chop off a piece of green ice in the cellar. Margarita heard him say something clumsy, the almost silly-sounding word "embolism," none of which meant anything to her. She saw the gold pencil drop from her mother's hand. Varvara Ivanovna's fingers were closing and opening, closing and opening, and her face was growing dim. Margarita screwed up her eyes and screamed in terror. Varvara Ivanovna sighed briefly and it was all over.

Margarita began to weep. Dr. Byrdin closed the deceased's eyes.

"Come away from here. Calm yourself."

But she was already leaving of her own accord, turning, shuddering in horror. No choices remained for her: no matter what, she had to marry Leonid Leonidovich. Otherwise all was lost.

Byrdin led her away to the small parlor. They gave her a pillow and brought her some water. The sky was already turning blue. A star hung like a raindrop in the window. The doctor's wife took Margarita's hand and searched for words of consolation.

Finally she asked sympathetically: "What is your patronymic, dear?" And Margarita blushed.

"Petrovna."

Neither one said anything.

"You go get some sleep," Byrdina said again.

"All right."

Margarita was left alone, and when the steps died down on the staircase and upstairs as well, a tremendous, hundredweight grief came crashing down on her chest, head, and legs. She lay there until morning without moving or crying and listened to first the birds, then the common folk, and then the ladies and gentlemen starting their day.

She came out of her room for tea. After considerable thought, she had wet down her curls. She seemed thinner now, and uglier. People bowed to her wordlessly, and a silence fell on the balcony, the kind of silence that sometimes fell in their Petersburg apartment in the evening, except that here in the garden the frenzy of the birds and crickets continued unabated and there were tears in her eyes.

"Please walk me upstairs," she said unsteadily, and everyone looked at Byrdin.

"First drink your tea. You look tired."

She sat down, picked up a piece of bread, and slowly began to eat and drink, gradually looking at the people around her.

Verochka was perched at the edge of the table. She had forgotten to wipe her lips and there was milk on them. Two other young women were sitting beyond her, next to Rabinovich. These were his daughters. The women's faces blurred before Margarita into a single, solid, reddish-yellow stripe; Rabinovich and Byrdin were the only men there.

"There's no one," she thought. "There was no point bringing my blue dress after all. Oh, Lord! What am I thinking about!"

Everyone looked at her and pitied her, although their tranquil life was going to be disrupted for the next few days. Before she came down there had even been a brief but excited conversation: "Have you heard the trouble there's been?"

"Just imagine! Who would have thought? To come to strangers. . . ."

"All this heat and now—a corpse. Why, that's positively a hazard!"

"And you can guess what's coming with it: the coffin, the incense, the singing. All that has a dreadful effect on me."

This was what the guests were saying, but the Byrdins themselves were somewhat at a loss. These were hard times, the common folk were intractable and arrogant, and the village was twelve versts away. The doctor chewed on his beard from time to time, just as his father, and his grandfather, and his great grandfather would have in their day. His wife was watching him, and although he was twenty-five years her senior, she still dared to have her own thoughts and arrive at certain decisions regarding Varvara Ivanovna's further sojourn in their house.

Margarita had heard that people die, but she had never seen death. She didn't recognize the hallway: large squares of sun on the floor, a blinding whiteness on the walls. Byrdina opened the door for her, and Margarita walked in, looking around timidly, but the doctor's wife had no intention of staying out in the hall. Curiosity was suffocating her.

The bed had been pushed closer to the window, as if the cooling air might do some good. The canvas blinds had been drawn shut, and through them fell a narrow, barely trembling ray of sunlight, which bisected the entire room as well as the dead woman's face.

Feeling Byrdina's gaze on her, Margarita began to cry. She got down on her knees and crossed herself. Then she went over to the head of the bed, noticed a spot under her mother's ear, and began crying even harder. As she kissed Varvara Ivanovna's damp brow, she saw very close to her own lips the sparse blond eyebrows, the dark lid of a sunken eye, and the mole with the little hair on her mother's left cheek that she had kissed so many times as a child.

"Come, dear," said Byrdina.

"No, no. . . ."

She touched two fingers to the crossed, purplish hands, which were bound together with a handkerchief.

"Who dressed her?" she asked, surveying the familiar gray dress. "And the shoes? You found them? They were in the suitcase."

Byrdina took Margarita by the arm.

"Let's go, dear, Margarita Petrovna"—she could barely breathe it was so stuffy—"Let's get away from here."

Downstairs, the doctor awaited them with some tweezers in his hand.

"My dear young lady. You and I must discuss what you are to do now. Sit down and compose yourself. Yes, yes, I know. This conversation upsets you. . . . Nadya, bring Margarita Petrovna some water. . . . It upsets me, too. All this is a terrible shock. Your mother had been quite well?"

Margarita began to sob.

"Now, now, calm yourself, calm yourself! Oh, how difficult this all is. And the most difficult part of all is that now we must discuss. . . . Is your father still alive?"

Margarita shook her head no.

"So you're completely, entirely alone? Drink some water. You and I must discuss what you are to do now."

At last Margarita blew her nose, took a sip of water, and wiped her eyes. Before her she saw the sun-filled garden she had yet to walk in, a path, a flowerbed, and on the bench someone's white dress with a blue sash.

"Who is that?" she thought. "Oh! It's Verochka!"

"So, what are we going to do now?" Byrdin repeated, lighting up his pipe. "You doubtless were hoping to take your dear mother to Petersburg?"

"Yes," Margarita said uncertainly. "Is that really impossible?"

"But you yourself arrived only yesterday. You saw for yourself what's going on with the railroads. And you have to obtain permission. This is the wrong time for that."

"Am I really going to have to buy a plot in the local cemetery?"

"That is precisely the point. Buy a plot, wait half a year for things to settle down, and then simply move the coffin to Petersburg. After all, it would be ridiculous to leave her in some far off village cemetery, days away from where you live."

"But that's obviously what I'm going to have to do anyway, isn't it? Is it far?"

"Twelve versts. Which means when spring comes, for example, you'll come and you'll have to travel over twelve versts and back with horses, only with the coffin, which may be the worst of all."

The doctor's wife brought in a pot of hot sweet tea on a trivet, took a jar of jam from the buffet, and deftly began to pour it out, drizzling patterns with the thick, dark raspberry stream. Flies buzzed loudly above her pink hand.

"What if we bury her here in the garden?" Byrdina asked.

"But could we?" Margarita wondered.

Byrdin stuck his beard between his teeth.

"We would have to discuss it with the priest, and

he would have to be paid. I have nothing against the idea, but for you that would of course be the best solution."

"And that wouldn't bother you?"

"No. Why should it? There's an excellent spot right at the entrance. You know, Nadya, where von Maach wanted to do his digging last year. Remember? And then of course it's only temporary. What's there to talk about?"

"I'm extremely grateful to you," said Margarita. "What would I have done?"

"Don't mention it. Of course, we could not bury all our guests in the garden, but one, especially during such trying times. . . . The situation must be resolved one way or another."

"How good they are," thought Margarita, and she began to feel that there was nothing dearer to her in the world than the doctor's shantung jacket and disheveled beard.

"We've acted unselfishly and humanely," the doctor thought at the same time. And he told the houseboy to harness up the wagon so that he could accompany Margarita to see the priest and order the coffin.

Margarita did not stir from Byrdin's side and so never did go out into the dense, fragrant garden, fearing the unaccountable temptations, weaknesses, and languors that had already begun to penetrate to her through the windows and doors of the house. The feeling of summer and freedom made her head spin.

III

The shepherd boy took a running start and rammed his soft head into the bull's hard belly. Flaxen hair tumbled out from under his louse-ridden cap, and his long whip dragged across the ground. At last the bull crossed the road and stepped off the road on his sharp, narrow feet, and Dr. Byrdin's wagon drove on. The shepherd boy took off through the tussocky meadow, ducking under the ruminating cows' bellies just for mischief's sake—he scarcely needed to bend over.

The first huts and wattle fences, a well, a pot-bellied boy covered in scabs, chickens, and the spirit of hereditary poverty. Old ladies' wrinkled faces that looked like they were made of black bread (their gray kerchiefs being the floury crust) appeared at the tiny windows. The street was deserted. Margarita was thinking, but about what? The ride through the fields had sapped all her energy. Enormous stacks of hay on shaggy carts had passed by so close and so quickly she could almost touch them, and the small men turned around and sometimes threw a pebble at her. Possibly in jest? Byrdin said nothing.

Ducks were quacking in the dirty slime of the pond. A little girl carrying a baby in her arms opened her mouth wide and dashed after the wagon as fast as she could go.

"Gimme! Gimme! Gimme!"

The doctor whipped the horse on. Now, though, barefoot, bare-assed, snub-nosed little boys and girls were running out of every hut and yard, their hands outstretched: "Gimme! Gimme! Gimme!"

Then two older boys, trampling the others, ran after the doctor:

"Sweeties! Sweeties!"

A post office and a school with a tumble-down porch flashed by.

The children began to drop back in the dust,

hurling curses at them; then stones started striking the body of the wagon.

That was when Margarita realized. She looked at the doctor in fright: "Faster, faster!"

He grinned and glanced back, then he turned a corner and began pulling on the reins. The horse stopped in front of the smithy.

The sound of measured blows emanated from the profound gloom. A red fire was crackling, and above it flickered large hands and a pale bearded face.

"Good day to you, Kuzma. Is Danila home?" asked Byrdin, jumping to the ground.

"You'll have to ask Danila about that," the voice replied, and the face disappeared. The man had turned his back.

Byrdin helped Margarita down, lashed the reins around a skinny birch, and walked past the smithy, past a puny garden, toward a peasant's hut. Both went up the stairs, leaning over to keep from hitting the tattered linen hung out to dry, and walked into the entryway. There was some kind of a barrel rolling around underfoot, and nearby a horse was chewing on something.

Byrdin knocked on the door, stooped, and walked into the hut. Margarita stopped at the threshold.

A workbench, swayback from long use, stood in the middle of the hut. At the table by the window, under a dusty icon, sat Danila, who was eating. His wife was serving him.

"Good day to you, Danila." And Margarita thought that this time the doctor's voice sounded softer and sweeter.

"Shut the door. Flies'll get in," replied the peasant, and Margarita stepped quickly into the room.

"We're here with a commission. I had a lodger pass away. What are you asking for a coffin?"

Danila gazed out the window.

"No. Can't take that on."

"Why not?"

"Got too much work as is."

"Still, though. We can't very well bury her without a coffin!"

"Without a coffin you say? That's true, you can't. . . . How about eight rubles?"

Byrdin waved his hand.

"You're out of your mind. Three rubles and no more."

Danila looked into the bowl, poured more porridge into his mug, and started tapping his fingers on the table.

"So, what about it?" asked Byrdin. "It's not my money. It's the young lady's. Give her a God-fearing price."

"Have a good trip," said Danila, almost insolently. "I hope your little gelding doesn't run off!"

Margarita tugged at Byrdin's sleeve.

"Will you take five rubles?" he asked, acting as if he were about to leave. Not that there was anywhere else to go.

"Nah. Today's not your ordinary times for us. They're gold. No one's going to take less than seven rubles from you for a birch coffin."

"Oh, all right. Make it, only be quick about it. If it has to be tomorrow, then tomorrow it is. We can't wait in this weather."

"That's a fact. If you wait that soul'll be long gone," said Danila soberly, almost gently. "But I can't have it before Thursday."

"Four days!" exclaimed Byrdin. "What do you think you're up to? How dare you mock me, you fool!"

"Comrade, I'm no fool to you," said Danila very softly. Then he chewed some more and asked in a sing-song, his eyes closed:

"Your gelding didn't run off, did it?"

At last they came to an agreement. The day after tomorrow, Monday, in the morning, he was supposed to bring the coffin. For some reason, Danila bowed to Byrdin over and over from the porch, and then, when the doctor and Margarita were already seated in the wagon, he ran out after them without his cap.

"What about the size! How big would your lady lodger be?" he shouted loud enough so the whole street could hear.

Margarita explained, holding her arm first over the ground and then over the wagon.

Danila nodded slyly. It looked as though he were laughing at them, not listening at all.

"Look, I'll get the priest for ten o'clock," shouted Byrdin, gratified to feel the movement of the bulky wheels rippling through his whole back. "Don't try to swindle me over this coffin!"

The wagon bounced along and rolled through the dusty village streets. The belltower's green onion dome and cross nearby seemed to jump up and down in the sunny, deep blue sky.

"How crude people have become," Margarita said pensively.

"Not for long. Everything will fall back into place again."

They had to push the jasmine bushes aside in the priest's garden. The priest's little girl was scrubbing the balcony floor. Buckets were clattering, banging, ringing. The priest, who wore a pigtail, came from the garden and stood before his visitors, hiding his hands and begging their pardon: He had been working in the earth.

Very briefly and quickly Byrdin explained the situation to him, and he understood immediately. It turned out you didn't have to bury a person in the cemetery. You could also do it in the garden, if that was all right with the gentleman doctor.

"Did you order a cross?" asked the priest. "Or are you going to make it yourself?"

They'd forgotten about the cross. The priest promised to nail one together himself.

"The times, oh the times!" he muttered. "You couldn't very well take the deceased back to the city, now could you? What do you say?"

He promised to be on time and bring the junior deacon with him and invited them in for a cup of tea. But suddenly Byrdin was sick and tired of Varvara Ivanovna's death.

"Oh no, we're in a hurry. The young lady is tired. The horse has to go to the station this evening."

Once again they were pushing the jasmine away from their faces and holding the stiff branches back with their shoulders.

They got back at six o'clock. Verochka came out of the garden to see Margarita. In one hand she held *The Era of the Great Reforms* by Dzhanshiev, and in the other a messy bouquet of buttercups, forget-me-nots, and ranunculus.

"Would you like to put this upstairs?" she asked.

"If you don't have water, I can give you my pitcher."

Margarita thanked her. She did not feel like crying anymore. She took the flowers and went upstairs. When she reached the hallway she was amazed by the unpleasant, frankly nauseating smell.

IV

Danila could just as well have not brought the coffin, but he did. Climbing down from the cart, he shook hands with everyone he met, casually counted the money, and just as casually hid it in his shirt.

They carried the coffin upstairs. It turned out to be six vershoks longer than the deceased, so they ran to tell Rabinovich, who was digging the grave. All red in the face and disheveled, Rabinovich was struggling with the spade over the round hole. He simply could not make corners. They sent for a peasant, a farmer a verst away, found him, brought him back, and handed him the spade. Rabinovich threw himself in the hammock and put a newspaper over his face.

Meanwhile, on the upstairs balcony, the ladies were lining the coffin with a length of sturdy calico. Verochka's mother was issuing instructions and occasionally sprinkling tacks into outstretched hands. The coffin looked like a long, narrow trough and was full of cracks and knots. On the lid someone with a woodchip dipped in ink had drawn a cross; the pillow was stuffed with straw.

Margarita kept walking round and round saying, "Thank you, thank you."

But no one said anything to her in reply.

Finally, they called in Byrdin, the two servant girls, and the cook, who lifted the deceased into the coffin. Then they took Varvara Ivanovna out onto the lower porch. It was cruelly stuffy and hot in the emptied room. An oilcloth lay on the bed, where it had been spread out the night before.

The priest arrived with his tinkly bell. The junior deacon went directly to the kitchen for some chunks of coal. Everyone assembled. The priest sat on the only chair, which had been brought out for him, and began talking about how, thanks be to God, the weather had been dry and they would be able to harvest the hay in peace, even if late. He asked the name of the deceased and began to put on his robes. The junior deacon passed out candles and lit the incense.

Margarita stood in front wearing Varvara Ivanovna's black dress (she did not have one of her own), which someone had altered for her. Her auburn hair gleamed; it was short in front and on the sides and right now uncurled and combed back. At this moment, her entire young, rosy pink face, her little eyes red from crying, her puffy lips and her freckles, were very much like those of Varvara Ivanovna, whose solid features death had restored to youth. Her pointed, upturned nose was almost maidenly; only her neck and hands were horrible to look at. From time to time, the ladies pressed handkerchiefs sprinkled with eau de Cologne to their faces.

The air was stagnant. Blue-gray incense smoke hung at eye level; there was nothing to breathe. The sun was getting higher and higher in the sky. Its rays had already fallen on the first steps of the porch, then singed Byrdin, who was standing at the edge, and began to move slowly toward the coffin. The birds had hidden from the heat, but big blue flies in a thick buzz kept flying right up to the deceased woman's face.

"Please don't let them land. Please don't let them land!" kept going through Verochka's mind, and suddenly she saw, from the very middle of the coffin, a stream of liquid falling between the two stools and onto the painted half of the balcony.

"Sins of commission and omission!" proclaimed the priest.

The stream ran toward a crack, spread, and puddled; the priest noticed it close to his worsted twill shoe. He said something to the junior deacon, who leaned toward Byrdin.

"We could use a basin."

A minute later the cook put a large, chipped basin under the invisible crack. The drops rang out abruptly and distinctly. Margarita could not tear her eyes away from them.

". . . Where there is neither sadness nor lament. . . ."

"Or this horror here, Lord," prayed Verochka. "This horrid dripping."

". . . But life everlasting."

And the junior deacon chimed in before the priest could finish and stretched his neck out as if his throat were parched from heat and thirst.

Everyone dropped to their knees.

"May her memory live on!"

Margarita began crying loudly—from grief, loneliness, and confusion: "Memory? Live on ? In whom? I don't understand. Only in me, probably, because there is no one else. But am I everlasting? It's all a lie. . . . Mama's gone. Mama's gone! When she was here, I had no use for her. She even got in my way when Leonid Leonidovich and I. . . ."

They nudged her gently and she regained control. They led her up to the coffin; she saw the paper crown and the paper icon in the hands she didn't recognize. She kissed her mother several times until she frightened herself and started sobbing once again at the top of her lungs.

The coffin was nailed shut, the priest shuffled down the garden path, and Byrdin, Rabinovich, the peasant farmer, and the junior deacon followed him down the steps, bent under the weight of the dead body and conferring volubly over what they should do.

The quiet heat of the large garden comforted Margarita. Her feet, shod in tall black boots—feet that had walked down the harsh Petersburg streets, which had been so terrifying of late—crunched lightly over the gravel of the garden path. The smell of flowers and honest-to-goodness country grass filled her. She took quick short breaths, her nostrils flared slightly. Her handkerchief was soaking wet, so she hid it in her sleeve.

Suddenly, a quiet wind touched the very tops of the plane trees and maples. Three drops of rain fell with a crackling on the foliage. In the thick shade where the grave had been dug they could hear the patter of rain beginning to fall. They set the coffin down beside the hole, which was haphazardly huge, rather shallow, and criss-crossed with innumerable roots. The peasant exclaimed: "Oh no! Not rain!" And just like that, as if he were completely alone, he trotted off to his farm. He was obviously worried about whatever it was he had left outside.

The priest started to hurry. Surveying the sky, the junior deacon sang faster and faster. They lifted the coffin on straps. A drop of rain fell down Margarita's collar and ran down her spine. Oh, if only it could continue! How wonderful! The wind, which had risen with warm force out in the fields, struck the garden and plowed through all its nooks and crannies. Byrdina ran back to the house to shut the windows. At last, the coffin dropped in, after which it took them a long time to pull out the straps they had used to drag it. Then they threw dirt on it. The junior deacon and the doctor grabbed spades impatiently because the rain had already begun to pound down on the canvas overhang. Everyone waited quietly until the mound was in place and the cross implanted. Margarita crossed herself.

When it was all over, the ladies dashed back to the house, lifting their wide white skirts. A long rumble of thunder rolled across the sky. Margarita left with Rabinovich.

"Mama, Mama," said Verochka. Her chest felt unbearably tight and she felt like crying. "How is she ever going to retrieve her next year? It's all going to be washed away today! The coffin's completely full of holes, did you see?"

"That's none of your concern," replied her mother. "Everything was done properly."

V

The woman traveling from Petersburg to Rybinsk to see her husband's relatives got off abruptly at Khomuty, taking her five-year-old daughter by the hand and dragging a basket tied with rope down the platform. Everyone in the train car was relieved. First of all, the little girl had cried the entire way, preventing anyone from getting any sleep, and secondly, the woman was a redhead and God only knew what redheads had in mind.

She dragged the basket to the station bench and sat her daughter down on the basket, a pale girl with dirty fingernails. The woman leaned over and wiped her daughter's face with her own handkerchief.

"Sit here a little while, Varya, and be good. Don't you cry or I'll leave you here by yourself and go see grandfather without you."

She unlatched the child's hands from her sleeve, went into the station, and asked a man wearing a railroad uniform if she could hire a horse for a few hours. She could pay well.

"Where are you going, comrade?" asked the clerk, suspiciously surveying her old cloth coat trimmed in dark fur and her dusty hat.

"To see Dr. Byrdin," she said. "Have you heard of him? About twenty versts from here."

"No, never heard of him." And the man scratched the top of his head. "Which direction would that be in?"

The woman looked around helplessly.

"When is the next train?" she asked.

"In about five hours."

"But maybe there's someone who does know? Maybe the peasants know?"

The clerk spat and went out. When he came back, he opened the door to the station yard and shouted: "Stepan Nikanorich. There's someone here asking about some doctor, Dr. Byrdin. Ever heard of him?"

But no one had.

"But might the peasants know?" The woman repeated the words and went out on the porch. Someone's cart was standing by the fence.

"Mama, Mama," the frightened little girl lisped as she struggled with the heavy station door.

A peasant came out of the cooperative store across from the station and walked toward the cart.

"Comrade, have you any idea where I could find Dr. Byrdin's place around here?" Margarita asked. "I need to go out to his place. It's about twenty versts from here, in the direction of some village, I don't remember. . . ."

"You mean Red Exposition, do you?" asked the peasant. "Only there's no doctor there. Oh, maybe you're wanting to know about the boarding house? Only there's no boarding house there. There was once, but not now."

"There was, you say?" Margarita became anxious. "That is just what I'm looking for: an old boarding house. Could you take me there and back here to the station right away?"

The little girl started whining again.

"Right now, as we're standing? Sit yourself down, child." And they agreed on a price.

"Am I going to the right place?" Margarita wondered, trying to recognize the fields that had once flashed before her eyes. But the season was different. This was May, and rye three vershoks high was a gloomy green under the lowering white sky. Then came strips of black, harrowed land, then swamp-meadows.

"At the twentieth verst, approximately," said Margarita, hanging on to the edge of the rattling cart. "At the twentieth verst there should be a turn off the road to the left, toward the house. You mean you've never driven by it?"

When he looked back at her, black wrinkles stood out on his broad, nut-brown nape.

"Never heard of it, don't guess," he said, with a sibilant 's'. "Lady, you may not see a house there. There was a revolt here three years ago."

"What do you mean I won't see the house?" Margarita cried out, and she hugged her daughter and the basket tighter. "That can't be!"

The peasant pointed to the left with his whip. A river ran through the cold, wet reeds.

"Recognize the river?" he asked gloomily.

Yes, Margarita remembered the river. She even thought she recognized the bridge's wobbly planking.

"I know, you want to take a look around the place," the peasant continued. "We get excursions coming here, too. I'm telling you, they revolted here, three years ago." And he lashed his horse.

Margarita didn't understand him so she fell silent. Varya was drifting off to sleep in her arms.

It was a long time until dusk, but the scant light was deceptive. It looked as if it would be totally dark in an hour, whereas in fact it was not even past noon. The road ran by under their wheels (Margarita was sitting with her back to the horse now), and other than the rutted, gray clay road, which was nonetheless moving and therefore alive, there was nowhere to stop, so quiet was the meager earth, so cold and miserable the harsh air.

Rooks landed on the cart occasionally and then sketched something incomprehensible and instantly forgotten across the puffy sky. From time to time the blunt thatched roofs of huts poked up near the distant line of the horizon. Solitary birches by the sides of the road curled up against the weak, damp wind.

The peasant turned to the left without a word. The road was mounded and grass grew between the ruts. The Byrdin plane trees rustled steadily, and Margarita recognized a portion of the broken wooden fence lying on the ground.

"This way, this way!" she said, and she waited for the broad roof and chimney to appear above the plane trees—even if there was no smoke. Above and between the planes, though, she still saw nothing but thick white sky.

The cart came to a halt.

"Where to?" said the peasant. "I don't guess you could turn around there!"

Margarita got out, taking Varya in her arms, which were still weak. But what was she to do with the basket? After all, the peasant could easily swipe it, just take it and leave. What would she do then? But the peasant got down as well. Would he go with her?

She was walking, leaning backward because Varya
was so heavy. Actually, there was no road, you just
had to go down a short way. There were some
bushes—thistle most likely—but by now it was clear
that there was no house. Bricks with corners broken
off were lying about, but no more than a dozen. Here
was a clearing—where the house once stood. The
earth was black and the trees were black. There had
been a fire here. The flowerbeds and paths had
merged into a dense, prickly grass, and the roots
had pushed up.

What silence! The garden, full of stumps and
nettles, had become tangled and sparse. Actually,
there wasn't a real garden. Trees poked up, but between them were only snatches of the same tiresome
sky.

Margarita turned in where there were green
boards lying around, nails jutting out of them. This
was where the gazebo stood. There had been so many
mosquitoes it was impossible to sit here with your
embroidery. Men had once walked by here carrying a
long trough on their shoulders.

Past the scattered, rotting boards there was more

rough grass. Varya suddenly woke up and started crying.

"Oh Varya, do be quiet now!" shouted Margarita, and then she looked back. Yes, the peasant was following her. He was curious.

And here it was. The quietest corner of the Byrdin land, the ravaged Byrdin garden: six mounds, six crosses in a row. An entire cemetery. Margarita came to a halt. You couldn't tell which one was Varvara Ivanovna. In the last seven years she had been hidden among rebels, or heroes, or simply other chance passers-by like her. Six identical mossy crosses and ground overgrown with goosefoot.

Cross herself? But Margarita wasn't sure there was a God. And the peasant might laugh at her, too. He was looking, his hands linked behind his back; he had had time to roll a fag.

"I'm telling you, lots of folk is dead and buried," he drawled, and his voice was deep and pompous. "Down below there's another ten graves or so, and across the river they dug a common one. I can show you, if you want."

Cross herself? She had forgotten how to think

straight lately. . . . Look, Varya has sat down on the grass. Now her panties would be black.

"Varya, do stop your crying," Margarita cried again, tears in her voice. "You're worrying me to death!"

Grabbing the little girl by the arm, she ran back to the cart, and her face was wet from her heavy tears, which were cold in the wind.

The basket was intact. The horse was nipping the grass with his old pink lips. Land striped with crops rose all the way to the sky. Oh, Russia!

Paris, 1927

Zoya
Andreyevna

Zoya
Andreyevna

I

Zoya Andreyevna nearly broke down in tears when she saw herself in the mirror. Her Assyrian feather had snapped and now hung down over her right ear; there were dark circles under her tired eyes, whether from the soot or exhaustion she didn't know, and the sleeve of her fur coat was coming out at the seam, allowing a clump of dirty wadding to escape. She slowly surveyed her skirt: the hem was ripped. True, that had happened when Zoya Andreyevna was getting out of the freight car and doing her utmost to conceal her slim, finely-stockinged legs from the men standing on the platform. She ought to have needle and thread somewhere in her things. . . .

Her suitcase lay open, and what her eyes first fell on was the packet of letters and photographs. She pulled them out, perched on the bed, and began looking through them. Here, she could put this post-card on the table, beside the inkwell, but not this one; it had an inscription. Actually, though, what did it matter? What's past is past.

She didn't have the energy to wash her hands or turn on the light. She sat in the dusk, in this cold and unappealing room, and felt exhaustion and self-pity surge through her like warm, soothing fire. Suddenly, tears began falling from her eyes and onto the scattered letters, and she collapsed forward onto the bed, her face buried in the blanket, overpowered by sleep.

Nadyushka tore herself away from the keyhole. "She's collapsed," she thought, and she ran to her mother without making a sound.

Kudelyanova was sitting by the window sewing. She sewed all the time and was always saying that she was on her absolutely last piece. From time to time she raised her plump head on its short neck and looked out the window at the bare trees in the municipal garden, at the roof of the bandshell where they'd played that loud music this past summer, at the corner building of the boys' grammar school. With every stitch she promised herself she would set her work aside. It was getting dark. At last, Anna Petrovna came into the dining room carrying a bowl of marinated vegetables. She lit the lamp and began setting the table.

Anna Petrovna was about thirty-five years old. She was slightly younger than her sister and had never married. Maria Petrovna considered her the second smartest person she had ever known (the first being the deceased Sergei Izmailovich Kudelyanov, who had been a district chief). What Maria Petrovna especially prized in her sister was the fact that Anna Petrovna never made a show of her intelligence in front of anyone, so that many people, including the deceased Sergei Izmailovich himself, considered her quite stupid. Every time she told him that she had an idea, he even used to say she was lying. To this Maria

Petrovna remarked that in order to lie you first had to be intelligent. In order to perpetuate Maria Petrovna's legend, Anna Petrovna endeavored to speak only in questions, demonstrating considerable ingenuity in this regard.

When Anna Petrovna walked into the dining room with the salad and lit the lamp, it all seemed amazingly appropriate to Maria Petrovna because it was at precisely this moment that she could no longer see her sewing.

"What's her name you say?" Anna Petrovna asked.

"Zoya Andreyevna."

"What, is she a Pole?"

"What makes you think that?"

"Zoya. What kind of an idiotic name is that?"

That very minute, Nadyushka walked in. She immediately sensed that she had come at the right time. If she was late at all, then not by very much. The discussion had come around to precisely what consumed her now. She stopped on the threshold, slipped her hands under her black school apron, and began to wait for an opening in the conversation.

Her tow head kept turning to face the speaker, as if Nadyushka were listening with the freckled nostrils of her not always clean nose rather than her long pale ears.

"She'll have her meals here you say?" asked Anna Petrovna.

"Just dinner."

"What about breakfast?"

"At her office."

"Which is where?"

"I didn't understand what she said. She said, 'I was evacuated with my institute from Kharkov. They reassigned us to the Europe Institute. . . .' Did you put the borscht on?"

Anna Petrovna nodded and began sprinkling vinegar on the salad and tossing it with a fork.

"She doesn't have typhus, does she?"

Yawning, Maria Petrovna plucked off the white threads that had stuck to her front.

"What's wrong with you! Don't scare me like that, please. I told her to take all her things off and beat them out, just in case. She promised she would."

Nadyushka decided this was her signal to jump into the conversation.

"But she lay down with her feet on the bed without undressing at all! And her hat—her hat has a feather on it, for goodness' sake!"

"Where did you see that?" her mother asked avidly.

"I looked through the keyhole, for goodness' sake!"

"Feather? What kind of feather?" asked Anna Petrovna.

"On her hat, auntie, and such a pretty one."

"Is she pretty, too?"

Maria Petrovna was silent. To her mind, the stranger was not unattractive. Nadyushka was hopping around the table.

"She's awfully stylish, for goodness' sake! She tore her skirt and keeps looking around at everything. She has great big eyes and she keeps frowning."

"I'm going to go look." Anna Petrovna could not restrain herself.

"You mean to say you're going to peek through the keyhole?"

As Anna Petrovna passed through the foyer, though, she stopped at the mirror to see what had happened with the new pimple she'd discovered on her chin that morning. Before she could screw up her face to get a better look, the doorbell rang. It was Tamara coming home.

When Tamara moved in with the Kudelyanovas (which happened soon after the death of Sergei Izmailovich, when Maria Petrovna decided to rent out rooms), Maria Petrovna was concerned that she not bring anyone in off the street to spend the night. More than a year had passed since then, but this had not happened. Often Tamara herself, of course, did not come home, but she never did bring anyone back and she paid her rent punctually.

In the morning Tamara woke up early and went into the kitchen to wash, dressed only in her nightgown. Then she had a cigarette, drank her tea, and woke up the student—who, like her, was lodging with Maria Petrovna—with her singing. She put on her silk slip and red dress, which was discolored at the armpits, and her gypsy earrings, and left for work. She had a job as a typist for the railway administration, where she kept fancy raisin pastries on her desk, as well as a powder puff, a nail file, and various other items that had nothing to do with work but that excited the imaginations of men beleaguered by office work and family happiness.

Before Tamara could take off her brightly colored scarf (she never wore a hat), Nadyushka and Anna Petrovna dragged her into the dining room.

"What's happened, ladies?" she yelped as her red dress with the big slit fell off one shoulder, exposing her threadbare camisole and her chest, which had love bites on it.

"We rented out the parlor," Nadyushka giggled. "A lady from Kharkov, very young, and so proud!"

"Well? Is she married?"

"She has a wedding ring, but the other one with the stone is on her pointer finger."

"Her pointer finger? Go on with you! Did you lower the price on the room?"

Nadyushka giggled again and spun around on one foot. Her slanted, pale eyes receded under the reddish puffiness of superciliary arcs. Anna Petrovna could see she hadn't found out enough. She hadn't questioned her sister properly.

Tamara could tell she wasn't going to get anything but vacuous exclamations from either Anna Petrovna or Nadyushka. Grabbing a piece of bread off the table, she ran into the kitchen to see Maria Petrovna. There, after putting a slice of the onion that had been cut for the gravy on her bread, she listened to Kudelyanova's more substantive tale of how the bell had rung in the foyer an hour before, a coachman had carried in an old, overstuffed suitcase, and wadding had poked out from the woman's torn sleeve.

The smell of onion, borscht, and roast lamb grew thicker and thicker: the hour of their succulent, aromatic dinner was drawing near. A dark, low sky looked in through the windows, and across it, clumping up, moved the December clouds, from northwest to southeast, tumbling bulkily one over the other. Downstairs, dilapidated cabs driven by haggard coachmen clattered down the broad, noisy street. People surged by in herds, the majority of them strangers to this large provincial town. The refugees, who had seen epidemics, devastation, and war at close hand, filled the town with horror and despair. They too surged by, these people, from northwest to southeast—from Kiev, Kharkov, and Poltava, through this cold and dusty town to the overflowing districts of Ekaterinodar and typhus-ridden Novorossiisk, only to turn back westward later, but this time to the shores of the devastated Crimea, where they entrusted their nomadic lives to small vessels that hurled wrenching but futile SOS's into the dark expanses of the Black Sea.

Meanwhile, though, in the midst of this Russian exodus, people were still searching for either a lost silence or a lost vividness, depending on their needs. They rocked the town with their wails and laughter. They raced from one end of it to the other: from the bespattered train station to the quiet private homes and suburbs, from the broad river, which cooled off at night, past the lights, cafés, and cinemas, to the distant and deserted streets that led out to the autumn steppe.

Somewhere, two or even three full days of horrific freight train travel away—even though the map said it was very close, incredibly, impossibly close—there was fighting going on. One side had fallen and retreated; one side had advanced, fanning village flames and exploding in triumphant abuse, to the typhoid-ridden district of white bread, English boots, and old men and women frightened out of their wits. The fighting was already approaching the bloody suburbs of Kharkov. Now the line of the front began past Lozovo, that same Lozovo where the windows of the Petrograd-Mineral Waters expresses had once sped by and the freshly inked pages of *The Azov Lands* had been tossed through compartment windows for early rising passengers.

Because of the silence and because the room didn't shake the way the freight car, packed with womenfolk, had, Zoya Andreyevna woke up feeling ever so slightly happier than she had all these last few nights and days. The room was dark, and outside the town's yellow lights twinkled. Zoya Andreyevna walked to the door, found the switch, and turned on the light. All at once it was dark and empty outside, and the soothing things so important to her right now suddenly appeared in the room: a bed, a table, a bureau, and her long-suffering, lacerated suitcase.

Zoya Andreyevna unlaced her boots and began walking about the room in her stocking feet as she changed clothes and tidied up. She knotted her thick, dark hair high on her head, buffed her nails with a chamois, and spritzed herself with the last of her Coeur de Jeannette, gazing wistfully at the bottle.

They called her to dinner at half past five.

"Fyodor Fyodorovich isn't here yet," exclaimed Maria Petrovna. "Anna, we really should wait!"

But everyone took their seats as usual. And as usual, no sooner had everyone done so than Fyodor Fyodorovich came back from the university.

He was quite thin, gawky, and grim. His curly hair stood on end, a shiny, deep red shock; above his large mouth and curling lips was a dark mustache. He surveyed the diners with a quick, stinging glance, stooped, and bowed. He grabbed a spoon with his hairy hands, which stuck out of his student jacket, wiped it with a napkin, and began to eat greedily without looking at anyone else. Every day Fyodor Fyodorovich wiped his spoon with his napkin, and every day Nadyushka watched her mother, as if inviting her indignation. But in her mind, Maria Petrovna had already come up with something much harsher: she would turn the student out of his room. These were fairy-tale times, and surely she could find a better-paying lodger.

Anna Petrovna walked into the dining room after Zoya Andreyevna had already sat down, so she was forced to suffer through dinner not knowing what the newcomer's skirt and shoes were like. On the other hand, she did have a good look at the white silk blouse with its open-work embroidery and tiny pearl buttons. The buttons and open work, as well as the watch with the leather band, stuck in Anna Petrovna's memory. She could have drawn it all on paper, if only she had been good at drawing. "That's all right," she thought. "We'll just see what happens next."

"So, what is happening in Kharkov now? Are there many people left there?" Maria Petrovna sang out, giving the signal for general conversation.

"Surely not everyone has abandoned their belongings and left for parts unknown?"

Zoya Andreyevna ran her eyes over their faces. She began to feel uncomfortable.

"Yes, of course, many people have stayed."

"Probably more who have children," Tamara spoke without addressing anyone in particular. No one had anything to say to that.

"So, were you traveling soft or hard?" Maria Petrovna began again, leaning into the steam over her full plate.

"No, not soft. We traveled in heated freight cars. For three days."

"With the men?"

"No, certainly not. The men rode separately. We had twenty-three women and their children in our car."

"Oh my!" Tamara marveled. "But however did you manage—"

Suddenly she stopped, took one look at Fyodor Fyodorovich, and snorted. Maria Petrovna and Anna Petrovna shook with laughter behind their napkins.

"—about food," Tamara finished up, winking at Nadyushka.

Fyodor Fyodorovich raised his head, looked at everyone, and seemed to notice Zoya Andreyevna for the first time. She looked at him with surprise and mild alarm, but the student's gaze slid over her face with the same indifference he conferred on everyone else.

She began staring at her own plate, at the piece of lamb in sauce, and the roast potato. Something bothered her about the way these people were treating her, so she began to eat quickly, behavior not at all in keeping with her outward appearance.

Tamara pushed her chair back and went into the kitchen for a pitcher of water, swinging her hips and bosom and throwing her head back as she walked. When she came back and sat down, she turned away from Fyodor Fyodorovich and asked: "Did you come by yourself or with your husband?"

Zoya Andreyevna smiled. Everyone could see she was embarrassed, and Anna Petrovna nudged Maria Petrovna under the table.

"No, I'm on my own," she said. "I don't have any

family. My husband and I have been separated for quite some time."

Once again Fyodor Fyodorovich lifted his indifferent gaze to the face and shoulders of Zoya Andreyevna, and Tamara was struck by the huge ring on her pointer finger. And suddenly she took a dislike to this fastidious, more than likely well-to-do newcomer, who in essence meant nothing to Tamara. As far as she was concerned, this lady, this damn prig, could go to hell in a handbasket.

Zoya Andreyevna did not raise her eyes again. After the lamb, a cold blancmange was served. Maria Petrovna took Nadyushka's plate and spooned a piece so deftly that Nadyushka got more than anyone else. Then Anna Petrovna and Tamara were served their blancmange, and then Fyodor Fyodorovich. Maria Petrovna asked:

"Would you like yours with or without milk?"

Zoya Andreyevna could not tell whether Maria Petrovna was addressing her or someone else. She replied: "Do you mean me?"

"Yes. You."

"No, I don't take milk."

Nadyushka exclaimed: "I thought so! Ha ha ha!"

Then for the first time Zoya Andreyevna became frightened. She leaned forward slightly, her eyes narrowed, and she looked at Nadyushka through her lashes: "But why?"

No one answered her. Maria Petrovna finished eating and folded her napkin into a wide silver ring on which the word "Caucasus" was engraved in Slavonic letters. She waited for Anna Petrovna to finish chewing, leaned on the table with both hands, and stood up. Then she went into the kitchen and saw the stack of dirty dishes she would have to wash, three more than yesterday, and she imagined Zoya Andreyevna once again the way she looked sitting at the table and remarked loudly, so the whole kitchen could hear:

"Isn't she the cat's meow!"

But Zoya Andreyevna was still in the dining room then, alone with Fyodor Fyodorovich, and although she knew for a fact that Nadyushka was standing listening right outside the door, she felt almost unconstrained. She surveyed the room closely and noticed two crudely painted plates hanging high on the wall, an upright piano with "Nadezhda Kudelyanova" drawn with a finger in the dust on the lid, and a graying palm next to the window. Then she stood up and walked to the door. It occurred to her that she ought to stand in the hallway and say "good evening," which could be construed to refer to both the student and her landladies in the kitchen, but suddenly Fyodor Fyodorovich turned toward her and looking right past her, at the door, asked: "Tell me, when are you leaving?"

She was taken aback:

"Me? I only just arrived today."

"I realize that. But I'm interested in knowing when you're leaving. Aren't you with the evacuation? You don't really think the Bolsheviks won't come here, do you?"

She fluttered her hands the way she always did at the most critical moments, when she didn't know how to respond.

"I hadn't given it any thought."

"Ah. Forgive me, then. I had assumed," he added, "I might learn something from you about the state of affairs. Kharkov has been taken."

"Is that possible?" she exclaimed and she pressed her hands to her bosom. "I hadn't known that this morning."

He regarded her coldly.

"Yes, taken. Didn't you only just come from there?"

She nodded.

"I have a brother there." Fyodor Fyodorovich stood up as well. "He hasn't written for a long time."

"Which regiment?" she asked, trying to express sympathy in some way.

"The N— regiment."

"The N— ? What a coincidence!"

She smiled and her eyes shone.

"Who do you have there?" he asked rather rudely.

"A dear friend," she replied simply, and once again a shadow crossed her face.

He fell silent, anxious to leave, but she was blocking the door and didn't notice him.

"If you would allow me to pass," he said finally.

"Please do."

She went out as well. Their rooms were next door to each other.

"Might you have something to read?" she asked suddenly, looking at him trustingly in the semi-darkness of the hallway.

"No, I don't have anything. On economics—here, textbooks. But that wouldn't interest you."

"A pity. You don't have Apukhtin? Or Akhmatova?"

He looked at her, amazed, and reached for his doorknob.

"Poetry?"

"Yes."

He bowed to her after muttering "good night" and was gone.

Once again the lamp was switched on. Zoya Andreyevna was left alone in her landladies' parlor, which was to be her home from now on. She was alone, but that neither disturbed nor gratified her. She had been alone with her very general thoughts of happiness for a long time and, of course, her very specific thoughts of romantic happiness, that she had spent so long searching for. She had someone in this world, and now she could look forward to thinking about him day and night. This someone had occupied her feelings for two years. Their parting had been a parting between two people who had promised themselves to one another.

But for a long time now the life of Zoya Andreyevna and the people around her had been intimately linked to something larger, the movement of elements whose trace, or rather, breath, had been especially evident in the last few weeks. Zoya Andreyevna had felt as if she were tied to the sails of a windmill: the sails turned and she flew out and up and then for a split-second felt solid ground beneath her, but she never could get a purchase on it and so would start turning once more. The war of '14 had separated her from her husband. He was unchanged when he returned, but she no longer loved him; he seemed a stranger to her, so she left him. Now the separation was different. Any day it threatened to lift Zoya Andreyevna out of her melancholy and worry and plunge her into utter despair. One barely perceptible change, and this could become a parting bereft of hope.

Zoya Andreyevna sat down at the desk. She felt unusually agitated. People were walking around and clattering dishes on the other side of the wall.

Tamara's voice said loudly: "So how's about it? Are you predicting the king of clubs for me or not?"

Nadyushka squealed something to general laughter: "There, that's just what she did. . . . So she said: 'Oh, you don't say! Kharkov has been taken! What a pity!'"

Right then Zoya Andreyevna heard steps and whistling in the hall—probably Fyodor Fyodorovich walking by. A door clicked somewhere, and a minute later she heard the sound of flushing water, and then the whistling again.

Zoya Andreyevna put her head on the desk, pressed her ear to it, and fell still. And suddenly, through the din of the Kudelyanova apartment, she distinctly heard other sounds, evidently coming from below, through the floor of the room and the legs of her chair. She heard music, the drowned out sounds of a piano and a man's voice singing something familiar, but what exactly she couldn't quite recall. She wondered at the tenderness of the melody and raised her head, but the music stopped immediately, of course. Then she covered her left ear with both hands (there was something childish in this) and again pressed her right ear to the magical desk that rang with distant sounds. She scrunched up her eyes and listened for a long time, until the singing stopped and the final notes of the piano died out in the distance.

II

The next morning broke altogether dull and dreary. Below, under the windows, hoofs thundered by over the cobblestones. The bustle in the house started up earlier than usual. A fine drizzle fell through the windowpane that had been left open in the dining room. Tamara took a long time to leave, singing, scuffling her shoes. She was waiting for Zoya Andreyevna. Nadyushka left for school wailing piteously. Halfway there she turned around and came back for her eraser, dawdled in the foyer, and finally disappeared. It was about nine when Zoya Andreyevna came out. She wanted to be calm, carefully wound up for the day, like a clock, but a melancholy filled her. "Oh, this isn't good, it isn't good at all," she thought privately. "What's making me so glum?

Haven't I known worse in my life?" Very erect and tall, if perhaps rather lethargic, she began gathering her things in the foyer. Tamara, a cheap cigarette stuck to her lower lip, stopped in the doorway.

"Good morning," said Zoya Andreyevna, and she began to hurry.

Tamara looked her over from head to foot.

"Are you telling me you dress like that on what you make from your job?" she asked, rocking on her heels and crossing her hands over her uncorseted breasts.

Zoya Andreyevna felt a shiver pass down the nape of her neck.

"This is from back before the war," she replied quietly, afraid she might say more than she should.

"Before the war?" Tamara repeated mockingly. "You mean you had more money then?"

"Yes." And Zoya Andreyevna reached for the door.

"Maybe you didn't work at all?" Tamara's voice was growing uglier and uglier.

"No, I didn't."

"And now, there, poor little thing, you do?"

"Yes."

"You mean you've suffered?"

There was laughter on the other side of the door. Tamara tumbled backward; someone had pulled her skirt from behind.

"Oh, Maria Petrovna, don't you go pinching me!" Tamara dodged her.

Zoya Andreyevna went out.

She descended the filthy stone steps. She was seeing spots. As she went outside, she made an effort to forget it all, but longing lay in her like a heavy lump. "Oh, what on earth is this!" she thought again. "Is this really any time to mope?"

The same insistent wind blew litter and swirled hems. The cafés were already jammed. Wagonloads of nails, hemp, and salt changed hands briskly. This was how civilians began a cold, windy day. There was no sitting around for the soldiers, either. They walked the streets, peering in the windows of food stores and turning blue from the cold. At that hour they ignored the women they passed, who pressed their muffs to their frightened faces. Sixteen year olds wearing leg wrappings clustered on the street like extras in some huge, unheated, dusty theater.

Others gathered by the entrance to the high school, where the tubercular school inspector vainly beckoned to them to return to classes. A battalion of recruits marched by with their songs, and behind them ran their girlfriends, weeping, all perfectly decent probably, not just any kind of girls, but with a recklessly crumpled look about them. The long, piercing whistles coming from the train station could be heard all over town, two or three at a crack. For five days blood-spattered trainloads had been pulling in and begging people to make just a little more room so that they could be with other people, so that they could take out the wounded, quarantine those with typhus, help small children get off and pull down their pants at the first handy booth.

Maria Petrovna heard those whistles and recalled her youth on the rail line. When everyone was gone and she and her sister were alone, she was drawn into Zoya Andreyevna's room with such force that she barely managed to drop the dustrag that she had been using to wipe the sideboard on an armchair and kick aside the kitten underfoot.

The air in the room had already grown soft,

warm, and fragrant, and Maria Petrovna, there in her own parlor, was instantly jealous. Her possessions seemed suddenly transformed. She went over to the bureau, saw the Coeur de Jeannette, the comb, the little scissors, then touched the robe hanging on the nail, and turned the backless slippers over with her foot. "She has everything," she thought. "Quite some little refugee!" And she peeked into the closet.

"Ah, so that's where you are!" Anna Petrovna exclaimed that same minute. "You set me to ironing while you come here? What do you think, I'm not interested?"

"Come now, please, don't shout." Maria Petrovna was embarrassed. "I only came in for a second."

"A second!" Anna Petrovna clapped her hands. "So where have you been looking? Where? You have to look in her suitcase, not the closet. What are you going to see in the closet? A dress form and a bodice. . . . You've got to look in the suitcase!"

They both crouched over the suitcase, but it was locked.

"There! You see? I was right!" Anna Petrovna exulted. "This is where you need to look! That's why she locked it. She has all kinds of things packed away in here."

No doubt about it, Anna Petrovna was a woman of exceptional intelligence. Oh, Sergei Izmailovich, Sergei Izmailovich. Why were you so blind?

Maria Petrovna looked at her sister with frank admiration. Anna Petrovna pulled a fine linen nightgown out from under the pillow, examined it, and stuck it back in business-like fashion; from the wastepaper basket she pulled a scrap of crumpled paper, smoothed it out on the desk, and deciphered on it someone's address written in pencil. She might even have checked the slop pail if Maria Petrovna hadn't suddenly lost her nerve: "Be careful, she's going to find out we've been digging through her things! Let's go."

"You go."

"Don't say that. Let's both go."

"You go and I'll be right along."

"Don't say that. Let's both go."

After their little spat they followed each other out, but in their heart of hearts they each decided to return. Suddenly there was a tension in their life that was beyond their understanding. Ever since the first hour of Zoya Andreyevna's sojourn in their house, their old life had felt violated. They sensed they may have fallen into a passionate segment of their existence, that in the general displacement, the universal alarm, the time had come for them, too, to live and act. Just as everyone around them was filled with anticipation of the end, so they too had begun to anticipate. Something told them that there were not two or three or four of them but no end to the people, no counting them—whether they had a needle or a slotted spoon in hand—gripped by the general hatred and vindictiveness.

Zoya Andreyevna felt lashed to the windmill's sails more than ever. She experienced a vague pleasure in greeting the people she had known for so long now in the ravaged rooms and hallways of the Europe Institute. In the morning, when she arrived at her desk in the corner, where her papers were spread out and journalists came and went, she felt closer to the stability she sought than she did in the evening chaos of the Kudelyanova apartment. Here were people who shared her fate, even if their distraught faces were greenish; their future would probably be identical to hers. She did not give the past a moment's thought or make any effort to locate friends from the past among them. These people sitting here, among the boxes of unsorted files and the tea-spilled desks, borrowing chairs from one another because there weren't enough to go around, were dearer to her right now than anyone else. Like her, every day they wrote letters that were mislaid at railway junctions; like her, every day they waited for replies. At four o'clock, the smoke-filled room emptied out. Zoya Andreyevna went home and from far away could already see eyes looking out the windows: Was she alone? Was she coming from the same direction? And at that moment, there awakened in her a melancholy which had never troubled her before, a mournful presentiment of something irrevocable.

At home she knew four pairs of eyes: Tamara's eyes, insolent, as if they were fingering everything she wore; the eyes of Maria Petrovna and Anna Petrovna, which slid over her face and arms like rats running over a corpse; and the lying, hating eyes of Nadyushka.

Zoya Andreyevna lived in a state of constant watchfulness. Waking in the night, she would listen for someone spying on her, someone sneaking up to take her unawares. In the evening, in the hallway, she was afraid that hands would reach out for her from behind the cupboards and trunks, or that a half-bared leg would suddenly be thrust out and trip her. "I ought to get away," she sometimes thought, "but where can you go these days?"

At dinner they would not leave her in peace. She felt as if they were tossing her around like a ball, grimacing, winking, and teasing.

"Are your parents alive, Zoya Andreyevna?"

"My father is in Moscow."

"Oh, is that so. A Communist, naturally?"

Or: "Have you ever been abroad, Zoya Andreyevna?"

"Yes, as a child."

"You must have had governesses, am I right?"

"Yes."

"And now, you're kind of like a governess your-self, aren't you—working and all. . . ."

"What about your husband, Zoya Andreyevna. Was he willing to give you a divorce?"

"We aren't divorced. That's difficult nowadays."

"Oh, is that so. That must bother you a lot, am I right?"

Fyodor Fyodorovich never said a word, but he salted all his food twice and sniffed every morsel. He lived in constant dread of the draft, and he couldn't have cared less about Zoya Andreyevna.

Nadyushka usually started out in a whine: "Mama, buy me a little medallion like that one there!" And she pointed to Zoya Andreyevna's amethyst locket.

"Where are we going to buy little medallions like that, Nadyushka! We're just simple people."

Anna Petrovna came to life: "We could never dream of little medallions like that. That's not for the likes of us."

Zoya Andreyevna thought, "What is this? How can I shield myself? It can't go on this way, can it?" But it did, day in and day out.

She might have left early and returned late, of course, locked her suitcase and not spoken to them, but she still couldn't change the basic facts, just as she couldn't buy a second-class ticket to Kharkov and leave, or telegraph Sinelkinovo: "I'm worried. Reply soonest when you can be in Rostov." The insistent northwesterly wind blew with savage force, hacking away at people, rocking Russia. The frightful storm twisted and turned Zoya Andreyevna as well, crushed her in its cruel paws, and bound and bore her away along with the fates of people, villages, entire provinces.

Twelve days had passed since Zoya Andreyevna's arrival, and once more people had started nailing shut the boxes they had scarcely opened and tying up baskets to be carried even farther. The trains passed by without stopping now. The town felt the front's proximity more and more and the human flood became heavier and heavier. Every evening when Zoya Andreyevna returned, her eyes searched for a letter in the foyer, but it was never there. Nadyushka was usually practicing the piano at this hour.

There was no letter that evening either, so Zoya

Andreyevna went to her room. She had been unable to get warm since the morning. The thought of leaving, of fleeing anew, did not frighten her, but she felt ravaged and suspiciously weak. When she walked she was afraid the wind would carry her off. It was cold and damp outside, cold and damp at the Europe Institute.

"Shut the door, please." She had been saying nothing else all day long. "Such a draft!"

Now, wrapped up in her scarf, she went over to the mirror and looked at herself. Her face was very pink, her eyes inflamed. "Yes, I do have a fever," she told herself. "I've caught a cold!" She dropped her head in her hands. How tiresome this was! Never, never before had she found life so tiresome! The trinkets on the bureau—shiny, glass and metallic—doubled and danced. Zoya Andreyevna could not tear her eyes away from them, so effortlessly and precisely did they dance. Then the unbearable, abominable smell of food wafted in from the kitchen. She ran to the washstand and leaned over the basin.

"Dinner's served, please!" shouted Maria Petrovna.

Zoya Andreyevna went out into the hall, tottering.

"I won't be eating dinner. I don't feel well," she said. "May I brew myself some tea?"

"Brew to your heart's content." Anna Petrovna whisked by. "But if you get hungry later, it'll be too late. No one's going to warm your dinner for you."

Zoya Andreyevna went to the kitchen, put the kettle on, and waited. There was heat coming from the burner, which she found pleasant, but the smell of oily residue drove her out. She rushed headlong back to her room. Beads of perspiration stood out on her brow, and her full mouth trickled saliva. She took two deep breaths, covering her eyes with her hand, and suddenly was shaken so powerfully that her teeth began to chatter loud enough to be heard throughout the room.

She threw herself on the bed and began pulling off her dress as she lay there. Then, feverishly, she crawled under the blanket and there, catching her breath, attempted to resist the trembling that was rocking her and trying to break her.

"What did you do—put the kettle on and leave?"

Maria Petrovna shouted. "Well, it's going to boil away and come unsoldered! Just look at—"

"They're ill!" Anna Petrovna shouted in reply from the other side of the door. "Our climates don't suit them!"

But Zoya Andreyevna stubbornly listened only to herself, arguing with her illness. She even found the strength to jump up and throw her warm scarf and coat on top of the blanket and lie down again.

Her head ached with a fiery pain. The throbbing in her temples matched the throbbing in her heart and the throbbing behind her knees and at her wrists. Her whole body pulsated with a painful, heavy throbbing. She began squeezing the insteps of her stiff feet in turn, to warm them a little. A chill ran down her spine and shoulders, but her face was getting hotter and hotter. Freeing one hand, she pulled out her hairpins and shoved them under her pillow. Her warm hair fanned out, covering the entire pillowcase.

When she stopped shaking and was experiencing an almost reassuring debilitation, she lay on her side, wrapped up tightly, pressed her knees to her chest, and tried to think. Her thoughts raced by, and she rejoiced in their distinctness, even if they were far from complicated. Her eyes rested for a long time on the objects scattered about the room. Next to her, on the nightstand, lay a packet wrapped in an old newspaper; gradually she saw it as well.

The letters jumped up and down in front of her eyes. "If I can figure out what that notice says," thought Zoya Andreyevna, "then tomorrow I will be well." She closed her eyes for a moment, then opened them again and focused intensely on the fine print.

"*Intell. gentleman mid. age,*" read Zoya Andreyevna, "*of means, lvs. music, sks. life companion under 30 yrs., cheerfl., modst., married or unmarried, refined.*"

"I read it!" thought Zoya Andreyevna, and her heart began to pound, but her head ached even more. "And now the next one, next to it." In her agitation she stretched her neck. Next to it was:

"*Widow, 28 yrs., pleasing apprnce., good char. refs., wshs. to mt. exemplary gntlmn. Goal—matrimony. Knws. langs., lvs. children.*"

"I'm delirious," Zoya Andreyevna whispered suddenly, falling back on the pillow. "Lord, I'm delirious. . . . I'm ill. . . . Now, what am I talking about? This is all nonsense. . . . I only need some sleep and this will all pass."

She shut her eyes. Inside her eyelids were bright pink and hot. "I'll think about him," passed through her mind. "Oh dearest, my dearest, where are you now?" And softly she whispered a man's name.

The light in the room stayed on all night. Several times in her sleep, Zoya Andreyevna asked someone to shut the windows and doors. The objects heard her words but pretended to be deaf. By the middle of the night, her hair was tangled and the blanket had been kicked aside. She tossed and turned in her sleep for a long time, until the tranquillity of a serious fever descended upon her. She answered the knock at the door with a barely audible moan.

"What did you do? Did you leave the electricity on all night?" asked Maria Petrovna. . . . "Oh my! You're very sick!"

She walked up to the bed warily.

"What's wrong with you? You're not contagious, are you?"

Anna Petrovna appeared silently in the doorway.

"You should come out, Maria. After all, we have no idea what kind of illness this is. She ought to go to the hospital."

Maria Petrovna took several steps back.

"It's not typhus, is it?"

"Well, of course it's typhus!" exclaimed Tamara, poking her head out of her room. "I told you yesterday. This means they were bit in the train car, but they hide these things from us."

The women dashed out into the hall and into the foyer one after the other.

"Get her to the hospital!" cried Maria Petrovna. "She's going to infect us all! Nadyushka, run get a cab."

Nadyushka dropped her satchel and threw her arms around her mother's legs.

"I told you so. In times like these you can't rent to anyone from the train station," smirked Anna Petrovna, and she fixed her hair in front of the mirror. "Now you see I was right. We're all going to get sick now."

"Not necessarily we're not!" shouted Tamara again. "Maria Petrovna, that's not how you get it.

You get it from parasites, and we don't have parasites, thank God. We don't go traipsing from one freight car to another, thank God. Send her to the clinic. Nothing's going to happen to you."

Maria Petrovna listened to her uneasily, grabbing Nadyushka by the shoulder.

"Wait up, wait up. . . . Nadyushka, it's too soon to go for a driver. She needs to be dressed. What are you so happy about? That you were right?" She was talking to Anna Petrovna. "Anything to irritate me! Tamarochka, you are right, of course, for goodness' sake. . . . But who's going to take her there? After all, she can't get there on her own. Did you see her?"

At long last, Tamara came out of her room. Her earrings sparkled and her face was powdered. Anna Petrovna took her by the arm with special tenderness:

"My but you look pretty today!"

Tamara smiled, flattered.

"Maria Petrovna, you're awfully inexperienced. You're ready to turn yourself into a sick nurse for a total stranger. Tell her to get dressed. Fyodor Fyodorovich can carry her downstairs. We'll all help, considering the situation. But she'll get there under her own steam. There's nothing we can do for her."

Kudelyanova walked slowly into the sick room. Wet snow was falling outside. It was nearly nine o'-clock. She walked toward the head of the bed and for a moment was distracted by Zoya Andreyevna's hair. "Cut it off!" she thought. Tapping her short fingers on her watch chain and tilting her head to one side, she said sweetly: "Zoya Andreyevna, you're going to have to check into the hospital. You have typhus."

Zoya Andreyevna opened her eyes, ran her tongue over her dry lips, and summoned up all the clarity she had left.

"Call a doctor, please. I've caught a cold. I most certainly do not have typhus. I'll be up and about tomorrow."

Maria Petrovna took a step back and picked up the dress lying on the floor.

"You're not dressed at all, Zoya Andreyevna? I'm telling you, it looks to me like you even removed your linen. Here's your dress. Fyodor Fyodorovich will escort you. He's a free man."

"Thirsty!" Zoya Andreyevna said softly.

"They'll give you something to drink there," Maria Petrovna said soothingly, signaling to her sister to close the door. "They'll look after you there. I can't. I have a daughter. I can't have sick people in my house. The other boarders could lodge a protest."

Zoya Andreyevna raised up on one elbow and turned pale.

"Call a doctor," she said, almost inaudibly. "He'll tell you."

Maria Petrovna shrugged.

"That's impossible, Zoya Andreyevna, quite impossible I tell you. By the time a doctor comes, anything could happen. Typhus is highly contagious. . . . Why don't you want to go to the hospital anyway? What are they going to do to you there, eat you?"

Tears fell from Zoya Andreyevna's eyes. They could see her wringing her hands underneath the blanket.

"You know very well," she whispered, "that they'll put me on the floor there with the typhus patients and the wounded."

"What's she saying?" Tamara asked Anna Petrovna, who was standing closer.

"She says it's true, a louse did bite her in the train car. 'I admit it myself,' she said, 'it's typhus.' "

Maria Petrovna suddenly walked right up to the bed: "Listen to me! I can't force you to go. You're not a child. Get up."

Zoya Andreyevna felt yesterday's insane shudder start up inside her.

"Close the door," she exclaimed weakly. "Oh, it's cold! Oh. . . ."

The blanket, warm scarf, and coat jumped about on the bed.

"Anna!" shouted Maria Petrovna. "Go call Fyodor Fyodorovich!"

She grabbed Zoya Andreyevna by the shoulders, turned back the blanket, and began pulling on first her dress and then her coat. Maria Petrovna wrapped Zoya's head in the scarf, but felt it would be beneath her to put on the shoes. Zoya Andreyevna did not resist. She just kept falling out of Maria Petrovna's hands like a big, soft, and very untidily dressed doll.

Fyodor Fyodorovich looked at Zoya Andreyevna's

legs, spread-eagled and clad only in stockings, and her arms flung across the bed.

"She isn't going to make it there, ladies. I don't care what you say," he said sadly and loudly, and was immediately embarrassed. "Certainly, I can get her into a cab, only that's the least of it. Just look at her. She can't even sit up."

Anna Petrovna, Tamara, and Nadyushka peeked out from behind his back.

"Who's going to take her there then?" Maria Petrovna became alarmed. "After all, we couldn't possibly. . . ."

"We need a man, Fyodor Fyodorovich. We need a man," Anna Petrovna cried affectedly.

Uncomprehending, Fyodor Fyodorovich looked around. His red hair poked out every which way, and his ruddy face was stupid and dull. Maria Petrovna turned to him.

"You need to do a good deed! The woman's alone in a strange town, Fyodor Fyodorovich. Considering what you pay us to live here, can't I ask you this one favor? I'll pay for the driver. The return trip, too."

Maria Petrovna opened Zoya Andreyevna's purse.

Fyodor Fyodorovich turned his whole awkward, bony torso toward the doorway.

"Go hail a cab," he said, and he went to get his overcoat.

Nadyushka opened the door to the staircase and rode the banisters down all four flights.

Tamara lit a cigarette as she surveyed the room. Maria Petrovna was standing by the window, waiting for the commotion to subside.

Fyodor Fyodorovich gathered Zoya Andreyevna up firmly in his long arms and carried her off. She was unconscious. Her legs swung freely, bumping into the chairs, and she let out a weak moan, pressing her cheek to the old fabric of his student jacket. In response to the swaying, she clutched his stiff sleeves.

Once they reached the sidewalk, she opened her eyes. The snow that fell on her forehead had brought her around momentarily. She saw at very close range a brass button with an eagle, and the button seemed very familiar, kindred, beloved, as if it were some- one's mark, the mark of a friend, someone she loved.

"Easy now, easy," said a voice coming from above. "Don't cry. We'll be moving shortly."

He sat her in the high cab and put his arm around her again. She sensed an amorphous calm from this final tenderness. How quiet it had become all around, how tranquil. Suddenly, though, she was thrown forward. The wind (oh, what a wind!) lashed at her face, chasing her with a howl and a roar. It's going to tear her in two, it's going to carry her away! Oh, hold her! Hold on to her, Mr. Student! Be a good man!

But Mr. Student, having put his arm around her shoulders, was looking back distractedly at the tall windows of the Kudelyanova apartment, where four faces were pressed to the glass, watching. How twisted, how terrible those faces were! Oh my. Oh my! He had never before noticed how ugly and distorted the glass in those windows was.

Paris, May 1927

The
Big City

The
Big City

It was autumn when I arrived in the city. A powerful, insistent wind raced through the streets. I could sense but not see an ocean on three sides of me (the city was on a cape)—over there, in the harbor, among the docks, along with the cruisers and giant freighters. From there the ocean hurled its rain and its hurricanes down upon the city. Shredded skies, heavy morning fogs that lay on the roofs, and people, so many people.

I was staying in a hotel downtown. It was as if I still couldn't get up the nerve to go further uptown, as if I might still be on the verge of going back to where I'd come from. The man on duty had only one arm and wore a great big medal that swung against his chest. It was a medal for saving lives. But whose? I kept wanting to ask him. I had so much to do and worry about right away, though, that I never did get around to asking. What lives? If they were ordinary lives, like mine, then just how did he go about it? But there was never a quiet moment for this question. I was looking for a job. I was looking for a refuge. Money was in short supply and time was flying. The unfamiliar mirage all around me seemed to share nothing whatever in common with my entire life and destiny so far.

There are attics and basements for men like me. I decided to find myself a room first. I walked up and down the side streets of the downtown area for a long time before I saw a paper sign: Room for Rent.

"Why don't you take a whole building?" the janitor asked me, and he led me to the four-story building next door. It was propped up by heavy boards leaning against the facade. "You could live here in peace until summer, but they're razing it then."

I declined, primarily because there wasn't a pane

of glass in any of the windows. You could see the cheerful but dirty wallpaper of the second-floor ceiling through the hole in the first, but that could have been patched easily. As I was walking out, I recalled a scrap of a poem:

I'd like to go
Where they hammer nails with violins
And feed the evening fires with flutes. . . .

Which is to say, for a moment I felt like a violin or a flute. It's a good thing no one could tell that I'd started feeling sorry for myself.

The other room, which I found at dusk, was all done up in cretonne—huge green flowers and pink leaves. The material covered the two beds. The short woman, her arms crossed high across her breast as if she were about to burst into song, pointed to one of the two beds and said: "That's where I sleep."

Before she said this she gave me a touching and actually rather humble look.

I bowed and walked out.

Green flowers and pink leaves, the street-level windows, and rain that fell suddenly, straight down, and very hard, not with a dancing, ingratiating slant

but rather with a confident sound: I'll strike everything, crush everything. That was what the evening
was like for me. "But you cannot, you simply cannot
let it get you down," I told myself. "You're a violin,
or a flute, or a drum, that fate has been beating on for
twenty years. Despair is prohibited. Spitting on the
floor is prohibited. What could that stranger ever tell
you? Jumping out the window will lead to no good,
too. *Pericoloso sporgersi.*"

The next morning I headed uptown.

On the tenth, fifteenth, twentieth floor of huge
buildings, right under the roof, they sometimes rent
out garret rooms. Cheap. Life goes on downstairs: elevators go up, dogs bark, telephones ring, perfume
wafts; people living in warm, spacious apartments
play games. But under the roof a corridor runs all the
way around the building and looks out at four different streets, and the numbered doors follow closely
one after the other: 283, 284, 285, and then, out of
the blue, 16, 17, and again, in the almost quiet of the
clouds, 77, 78, 79, a landing, a turn, the service elevator descending with someone's trunks, a trash re-
ceptable as big as the Tsar Bell in the Kremlin but

without a piece knocked off, a light burning, the corridor ahead a couple of hundred yards long. A fire extinguisher, a hose, a crawl hole to the roof. If you opened it at night, in would rush the starry gloom, the chill of coming nights and days, and that same autumn wind, that same nearby ocean that rings the city, droning, and the rumble of the streets somewhere below, an incessant, fiery rumble.

I paid a week in advance and moved in that evening. I locked the door. I wasn't locking myself in; I was trying to lock the world out. And then another world, many times greater than the first, welled up inside of me, here, within these four walls. This world had an ocean, too, a city, a sky, an endless stream of people walking past me, rain, and wind. Besides these, though, it also had the memory of a journey: the sun, the Italian town where you and I stayed not so long ago, the fragrant shore where toy boats strung with lanterns sailed by in the evening, and the pink steam that hung over a volcano as old as the universe. At first you thought the potted palms in the hotel garden were artificial, but one morning a flower bloomed with a light pop.

All of this was mine, needed and beloved by me alone, alive only inside me. I was trying to lock out what belonged to everyone. That hum and rumble you could hear from far away, but you didn't have to listen to it. I washed up, had a bite of cheese, bread, and an apple, and lay down on the narrow, hard, but clean bed. Suddenly, reflected light began streaming through the uncurtained window—onto me and everything around me.

The red needle of a distant skyscraper was reflected in the sink, and a blue flame fell on the face of my watch. Something orange played with the door lock, and the ceiling suddenly looked as if it had been sliced by a long ray. Something flickered in the corner. I didn't guess right away that these were the buttons on my jacket, which I had dropped on the chair. It was as if an airplane had sailed over me from wall to wall, nearly grazing me with its propeller. A precise raspberry circle ran across the ceiling (a fire truck racing somewhere with its distant clanging). God knows how many times it had already been reflected before flitting in my eyes. A lilac spark lay on my chest for a few moments before shifting to the windowpane and staying there. It felt as if, despite the fact that I had settled on the eighteenth floor, the entire city was running down my shoulders, face, and arms, as if the streets were passing not somewhere below but here, across and through me, and blinking in my eyes with dozens of reflected lights.

I woke up after noon and saw that the room needed painting. I got dressed, went out into the corridor, locked the door, which bore the number 199, and rang for the elevator. It was the service elevator, which was the only one I was allowed to use. A man in a gray livery jacket and frayed trousers greeted me politely. I asked him whether I could go up and down myself without bothering him. He said that was quite impossible, but that if I liked I could use one of the other two elevators at the end of the corridor, where the trash bins were.

"What a large building," I said as we flew down. "There must be twenty entrances."

"Twenty-four entrances," he said, "forty-two elevators, and 3,656 tenants."

"Exactly 3,656?" I exclaimed. This figure reminded me of the flowering palm.

"Exactly," he replied.

Before buying paint and a brush, I spent rather a long time walking around the streets. I had arrived a week before and already was starting to understand a lot and guess even more. The diversity of faces that flashed by astonished me. There was no majority in this city; all the people were unusual. This was what distinguished it from the cities I had seen before. What was even more amazing was that I could not forget for a second that all these millions of women and men—or else their fathers, or their grandfathers—had taken the same journey as I had. So not only was there no majority, but people's pasts were not equal either. There was one more circumstance that surprised me in an odd way, but I'll get back to that later.

I bought paint and a brush, returned to my room, and began painting the gray door a pale green. Immediately, I started to sing. The paint went on evenly and smelled of drying oil. I painted and sang, trying not to splatter the floor or myself. I began to get the feeling that I could live here, that in this room—as one of 3,656 tenants in this building—I was in the right place, and that after the first night spent here something had insinuated itself into me, filled me, laid down with me in bed, and was now pulsing through my veins.

I painted and sang—and thought, meanwhile, about how, if you were with me, you would be standing next to me and saying, Isn't there an apron you can put on? You'll smear yourself and ruin your only trousers! And suddenly, as if in revenge for that thought, I let a fairly long drip that reminded me of the shape of a willow leaf fall on my knee.

I rubbed the spot for a long time, but it wouldn't go away. I stopped singing and scratched distractedly at the material, which had worn thin over long years of wear. The spot doubled in size. Now it was huge, dry, and white. And suddenly I remembered seeing painters working by the stairs at the end of the corridor when I was going out in the afternoon for paint. And painters, according to my lights, ought to have turpentine.

"Maybe here the painters have something even better than turpentine," I told myself, as I wiped off the brush and smoothed my hair. By the way, about turpentine. The fact that my first childhood memory is connected with it has left me with a special, though rather unusual, feeling for turpentine all my life.

I was not yet three. One evening I came down with a cold. My mother (quite young and ever cheerful) ran out to the pharmacy and gave me a sweet, tasty medicine. I had to take it every four hours, for my cough. In the night I woke up and saw my mother standing over me, smiling, rosy with sleep, wearing a long white gown trimmed in lace and offering me a spoonful. I swallowed the sweet, tasty stuff, holding it for a second in my mouth preliminarily. Suddenly I saw the vision with the empty spoon in her hand disappear, melt away. She'd fainted. My mother was lying on the floor, unconscious, having realized she had given me not my medicine but the turpentine she had rubbed me down with before bedtime.

They wouldn't let me fall asleep. The doctor loomed over me like a tall tower and interrogated me. Did it burn? Hurt? They had me drink hot milk. "It was very tasty," I said. "Give me more." If I were not afraid of being misunderstood, I would say that this memory of the swallowed turpentine lent a certain cast to my entire life.

Hastily putting myself in order and buttoning my top button, I went out, locked the door, and went to the left, toward the exit: 198, 197—all the doors were identical. At about 155 the corridor took a turn, and there were 12, 13, 14. And indeed, on the broad landing, where huge, dry mops were stood up on end, two painters, one black and one white, were stroking the wall with broad brushes, and the paint was coming out nice and even, without any bubbles.

"Pardon me," I said. "Could I have a little turpentine? You see I . . . by accident. . . ."

I showed them the spot.

The black man and the white man both looked at me and at the spot and turned away, each continuing to stroke his own corner deftly and evenly.

"Turpentine, please," I repeated.

The black man tugged at his nose.

"Here's the thing, sir," he said, but as if he weren't addressing me. "There's a man living in room 274 who has what you need. At least that's what we've heard. But we don't have any turpentine. Am I telling the truth or what?"

The white man let out a sound that expressed sympathy.

"There's a man living there who sometimes definitely has what you need. Or so we've heard," the black man continued, "and that's why I'm telling you. Go to his room and knock on the door as hard as you can. You'll find your turpentine there, if what we've been told is true. Am I telling the truth or what?"

Once again the white man emitted a sympathetic grunt, and it seemed to me that all this might very well be the truth. I thanked him and continued on. Soon the corridor made another turn; it doubtless ran all the way around the building.

How many times I turned with it I don't remember anymore. I was looking for door 274. Once I thought I'd found it: there was 271, 272, 273, but then it started back with single-digit numbers. I figured at some point I'd reach my own room this way, but when? And what awaited me in the meantime?

The ceiling lights were switched on. From time

to time I heard sounds coming from behind doors, first here, then there: water flowing, someone arguing, a sewing machine running, hammering. A child beginning to cry. According to my calculations, at least a quarter of an hour had passed and I was still walking and walking—and then suddenly I came to an impasse, or rather, a staircase that spiraled downward. I took a look, leaning over the railing. And I was drawn down.

What I saw astonished me. It was a covered street complete with stores, offices, lamps, mailboxes, shoeshine men. The only thing it didn't have was automobiles, and the shuffling of feet over the stone slabs reminded me of that little Italian town. But that's beside the point. Now that I'm used to it all, I know that sometimes in the huge buildings of this city, on one of its upper floors, they set up something resembling a street. Now I certainly see nothing strange in the fact that, for the convenience of the people living in the building, a post office has been opened below me, that a tobacconist, a hairdresser, a shoemaker, a pharmacist, and a baker have opened their own establishments. That first time, though, it all seemed to me like a fantastic dream, and for a moment I doubted that I myself had rented a room on the eighteenth rather than the second floor. The ceiling, however, told me that I was not outside but inside the building. A little girl was standing in front of a bookshop window scratching the top of her head. A fat man sprawled out in a chair watched his shoes being shined. The sounds of some song came from a radio store and the smell of pastries from the little blue candy shop.

I didn't walk down that street. I ran. Shops alternated with offices. I noticed a sign for a dentist. There were homes and land for sale—prairies, riverbanks, and lake shores. Here was a domestic employment bureau. Round lamps hung on iron rings, a mailman dashed by, two women jabbering and laughing looked straight at me. And suddenly I came to a spiral staircase. Whether it was the same one I'd come down or a different one I couldn't tell, but I ran up it. I ran up and recognized a familiar series of doors, which I walked by quickly, checking the numbers.

After about twenty minutes I began noticing that

I was getting close to the door I was looking for. Now the numbers were going backward: 277, 276, 275. At last! Door 274, no different from the other doors, right in front of me. Except that it was ajar.

Knocking cautiously on the doorjamb, I took a deep breath. No answer was forthcoming. I knocked once more and quietly walked in. The room, twice as big as mine, was piled high with furniture. There was even an armchair on top of the cupboard, which was open wide and spilling out bits of old material, evidently upholstery fabric. Pictures were hung all the way to the ceiling. One showed a ship in full sail over the stormy sea. Old picture frames were stacked in a corner. A marble bust of some Roman stood amid the rubble. The entire right-hand wall was taken up by a broad old sofa upholstered in a Scotch plaid, and on it, calmly, in a comfortable pose, as if he were expecting someone, sat the master of this room, a man nearly sixty. He was smiling. His face was pleasant— once it had been handsome, but the features were flabby now, the eyes bloated. They were big, dark, somewhat sad, but good eyes, intelligent eyes, under heavy dark lids, in a soft and good face.

His hair was in disarray and longer than men ordinarily wear it. He had on an old—very old—loose jacket and slippers on his feet. Once again I looked him in the eye and bowed slightly.

"Pardon me," I said, almost not feeling shy, although at that moment my arrival seemed rather odd even to me. "The painters told me—they're working over there—about turpentine. . . . You must be an artist, right? I have this spot here, and I'd like. . . ."

Still smiling calmly and cozily, he took a bottle off a shelf. "People live so amazingly," I thought, "and each in his own way. Especially during the day. At night, all kinds of lights must find their way here, too."

The man moistened a clean rag with turpentine, squatted with a slight crackling of bones, and wiped my knee. The familiar smell tickled my nostrils. The doctor had towered over me. His glasses had gleamed in the dark sky and his beard had raced by like a cloud. "That's very odd," he said angrily and for the umpteenth time he shrugged. And my mother, who had put on some kind of skirt, was leaning on to the wall to keep from falling a second time. I never again saw her seeming so serious. "It's absolutely incomprehensible. The child must be made of pig iron!" I was sitting on the bed and looking at them avidly in hopes of a second spoonful. "My little puss, my chick, my sweetkins! Throw up! My darling!" my mother pleaded. I shook my head. I didn't even understand her murmurings, why she was begging me so in such humiliating fashion.

The man straightened up with more slight crackling. The spot was gone.

"What did the painters tell you?"

"They told me to knock as hard as I could!"

"What fools!"

"But your door was ajar."

"That was their idea of a joke. I never close it. Whenever someone needs to, they come in."

"What about at night?"

"I shut the door at night."

"What does your window look out on? May I take a look?"

While I was making my way over to the window, he said: "Except that I'm not an artist. I'm a framer and upholsterer."

I looked out the window and saw roofs and sky-scrapers that were already familiar to me. In the dusk of the gathering night, lights glowed, advertisements flashed, the red needle, my nocturnal raspberry friend, reached into the high and cloudless sky directly in front of me. Above it an airplane with a blue star on its tail flew by, and some word blinked and pulsed well beyond the bridge.

"Take a look through my binoculars," the man said, handing me the heavy old instrument by its strap. "A marvelous view! Over there, between those two smokestacks, sometimes you can see the sea, and a little more to your right you can see the zoo."

I brought the binoculars up to my eyes, twirled one little wheel and then the other. And suddenly a block away, in a lighted window that hung in front of me in the sky, I saw a room and two little boys in it. They were standing at the table, and each one had a knife in his hand. Both had just cut their own arm and were trying to drip blood on the piece of paper that lay in front of them. One of them was wearing a feathered headdress and the other a Mexican mask pushed back on his forehead. I looked higher up. A woman was attempting to open the closed drawer of a high narrow bookcase, trying to find the right key. She was in a dreadful hurry, and in the lefthand corner of the room, I couldn't hear it but I could see very distinctly a record player playing. The record was spinning.

In a neighboring window a body was lying on a sofa, and a dog was circling it mournfully. The sad, elegant, pedigree borzoi shuddered and looked out the window, so that our eyes actually seemed to meet for a moment.

"What kind of binoculars are these?" I said, finally swallowing my saliva. "What on earth is this?"

The man smiled at me trustingly and gently: "This is nothing! There are even better ones. Once I held in my hands a gadget they say a German saw Petersburg through in '42, and then, a year later, the pyramid of Cheops."

I looked again. The boys had signed their names in blood, the dog was looking at me as if it were made of stone, and the record was still turning. A floor lower a drawing class was in session, and lower still two couples were dancing in the semi-darkness.

More to the left, where the façade of that distant building ended, through the gap, the harbor lights twinkled on a white steamer that had sailed out to sea. The dark blue water was flooded with violet reflections, black smoke hung perfectly still, and beyond it you could just make out a flat island with a tall radio tower. (Was that the green eye that had spent last night on my shoulder?) The flat island turned muddy, and beyond it was the real and boundless ocean.

I bent over a little, and there, far far away, under the stripped trees of some park I didn't know, where white, round street lamps shone with hundreds of lights, in the autumn gloom, I saw wild beasts behind the bars of their cages. I saw a guard signal to a tiger to go through a small low door, which it did, and the door dropped. On a sand-sprinkled clearing, a pensive, two-humped camel laid his shaggy little head on the back of another.

A large heavy hand dropped onto my shoulder. I remembered where I was. "Now he's going to ask me to leave," I thought.

"This is a very entertaining activity," said the

man, and at close range I now saw his tired, dark brown eyes, and his thin but broad eyebrows tinged with gray. "You can look and look until your eyes go funny. I don't do it anymore. Maybe sometimes at night, when I can't get to sleep, if someone has an uncurtained window."

Could he have seen me yesterday from this window? I thought at that moment. Is that possible? Of course not. That's impossible. We can't see what's going on in our own building.

"Won't you have a seat?"

There was now a chair behind me, a lamp had been turned on, and a glass had appeared in front of me. Our conversation flowed as if we had known each other for a long time, a little bit about everything: beauty and the greatness of this big city, where to look for work, how to use the telephone booth by the elevator, and where to buy bread and milk. A few precious words about insignificant matters. I never knew I liked precious words about insignificant matters, and a quiet voice and big hand pouring me wine, and the attentive expression with which he listened to me. I felt good. I felt untroubled and warm.

I told him I was happy to have met him, that he had amazing, unusual, mind-boggling binoculars, that if you really tried, I was sure, even from here, you could see the pyramid of Cheops through them.

And once again I walked over to the window.

The dog was gone. So were the boys. The ship had gone around the island and had probably been sailing at full speed for a while. Certain windows, though, windows that hadn't been there before, were now lit up here and there. I began looking. A ceiling light was burning in a narrow room. There was a table and a chair. And some kind of bucket. A man was sleeping on the bed. There was something familiar about him. No, it just seemed that way.

A woman opened the door slowly and walked in. She stopped, looked, and walked over to the sleeping man. The bucket was full of light green paint and on top of it I had set down my brush. You came up to me and put your hand on my chest, your skinny, ever cool hand, and a moment later you took it away and lowered your eyes to me. You were wearing the same dress you were wearing the day I left. It was too long for you, but there was no time to deal with alterations or to mend it at the collar, where it was coming apart at the seam. A lock of your hair fell on my forehead, you kissed me, you began to cry. You were with me. You were telling me something. It was probably about "us." You were always talking about "us." Not "you," my happiness with you, but "us." It's not when people switch to the familiar form of "you," it's when they switch to "we." "You" can be taken away in parting to the end of the earth, but not "we." It breaks down the moment people part.

"Finish your wine," said the man whose guest I still was. "I'm sure you'll find a job in your field very soon, and in general I can see you are an educated man. You know how to behave in society."

"Forgive me," I said, hastily making my way to the exit. "I've overstayed my welcome, and I came without being introduced and with a request right away. I don't know how to thank you."

"There, you see?" He smiled. "Didn't I say you were a polite, educated man? Stop by any time. You're always welcome. I light the fire on Saturdays and my girlfriend comes over. I'll tell her to bring a lady friend for you. She's a young girl and works as a cashier. We feed the fire with that old harp lying in the corner. I've already sawed it in two."

I stepped out into the corridor. My door turned out to be almost next to his. It was locked, of course, just as I had left it. And inside, of course, there was no light on—when I went out it was still daytime and I'd had no reason to turn it on.

Now I can say something about that observation I made when I went out that afternoon for paint. I realized then that every person brings whatever he can to this big city. One brings the shadow of Elsinor's prince, another the long shadow of the Spanish knight, a third the profile of the immortal Dublin seminarian, a fourth some dream, or thought, or melody, the noonday heat of some treasure, the memory of a snow-drifted grave, the divine grandeur of a mathematical formula, or the strum of guitar strings. All this has dissolved on this cape and formed the life I plan to take part in too from now on. With you, who are not here with me but alive in this air I breathe.

1952